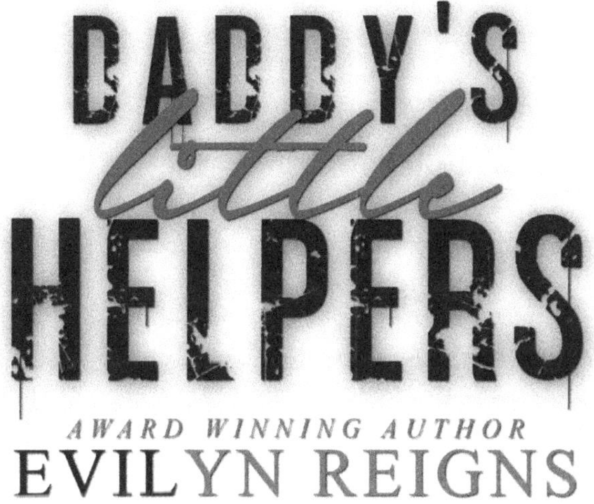
DADDY'S
little
HELPERS
AWARD WINNING AUTHOR
EVILYN REIGNS

Daddy's Little Helpers

Editing and Formatting: Beth A. Freely

Cover Design: Dark Water Covers

Also by EVILyn Reigns

Abnormal Carnage

Little Black Book

The Gem Collector

Author's Notes

Daddy's Little Helpers

Revenge will come when least expected, icy, cold, and with a smile.

I saw a news story a couple of years ago. In my home city near Houston, Texas, a sex trafficking ring was found and dismantled, with many men and women sent to prison. I thought I lived in a safe community. Turns out there is no such thing. Trafficking is found everywhere.

A story began to brew in my head. Young girls who survive trafficking are forever damaged physically, mentally, and emotionally. But what if they were able to take back the pain? What if they were able to heal through vengeance? This is when Denver grew a voice, and her story began manifesting. EVILyn had woken up, and she was pissed.

Stats:

Texas is the second highest state for trafficking, with 234,000 people trafficked per year. People, as in girls and boys.

Out of that number, 79,000 are minors. Only 987 cases where the perpetrators were caught and convicted. In this practice, over 200 babies were sold last year.

These stats are from the National Trafficking Hotline.

Out of all these numbers and all these children, three young girls escape and plan to take back justice for all the wrong done to them.

They are ***Daddy's Little Helpers***.

This book is dedicated to all the people who are a victim of sex trafficking. I am your voice, and I am giving you revenge.

Chapter 1

Thunder rumbled across the black sky, lightning showcasing the small country bar hidden behind a crop of trees in the small town of Bellville, TX.

The slow ballad playing from static-filled speakers had her swaying under the dark, black sky as she stared at the rickety sign swaying dangerously in the storm wind that blew through the town. Her torn skirt threatened to fly up above her knees, fingers of the strong air exposing her to the elements, her moon hiding behind the storm currently enveloping her mind, her heart.

Taking a deep breath, she began to walk toward the entrance, praying for relief from the storm outside and her life.

Her breasts began to tingle, milk dripping from her engorged nipples as blood trickled down her legs, pain radiating through her entire body as she stumbled up to the open doorway of the bar.

Claps of thunder made her jump as sheets of icy rain poured onto her trembling body. A whimper escaped her backpack as she adjusted the shoulder straps. She ran into the bright bar, the door slamming behind her with a loud crash, heads turning toward her when she accidentally interrupted the young female singer.

An infant's cry from her backpack pierced the now silent room as she collapsed to her knees, relief shattering her fears at finally finding shelter from days of walking.

"Don't let him find me. He'll find me!" She screamed as her vision wavered and the room spun under her feet, pinpricks of light exploding behind her eyes as she felt herself fall toward the floor.

Waking up, she closed her eyes against the bright sun currently streaming in through the little window above her bed. Her vision was milky with sleep, and she rubbed her eyes to clear away the crust forming on her lashes. Looking around, she realized she wasn't in her cell and sat up in bed, pulling at something in her arm. She looked down in confusion at the IV pumping clear fluids into her vein. Dust particles danced in the sunlight as she stared into space, trying to remember how she got there.

"My baby!" she yelled as she felt her stomach, finding a soft skin flab where her once hard belly used to be. A whimper beside her had her whipping her head to the side and sighing in relief at the sight of her small, newborn infant lying in the bassinet. Bright blue eyes connected with hers as the baby's face twisted, a sure sign that a cry was about to begin.

She didn't know where she was, so she quickly picked up the baby and brought it to her chest, hissing as the infant latched onto her sore nipples. Tingles gathered in her breast; her letdown burned as her child suckled in hungry anger. Footsteps sounded outside the room. Fear had her sinking lower into the mattress, trying to hide herself and her daughter under the covers. She didn't know where she was, only that she barely escaped her captivity before giving birth to her child.

The door swung open to a tall woman. She walked in with a tray holding a steaming bowl. The comforting smell of chicken soup and bread had her stomach growling in discomfort.

"Oh, you're awake!" the woman said as she looked at her in surprise. Her black hair was pulled into a tight ponytail, with long, unruly curls spiraling down her back and over her shoulder. Dark brown eyes reflected the sunlight that shone into the room as she wriggled her nose in disgust.

"I think your little one there made a smelly deposit," she said as she walked over to the nightstand, sitting the tray next to the young woman. The baby let go of the breast and began to cry in discomfort.

The woman reached out for the baby and carefully picked her up, much to her squeak of disapproval.

"Hush, I ain't going to hurt your baby. I'll burp her, change her, lay her back down while you eat. You need the calories."

The young woman watched the brunette tenderly care for her baby and decided to eat while she watched. Honestly, she had no clue how to care for a baby and probably needed to watch to learn.

As the other woman began to pat and rub her baby's back, she leaned back and rested her eyes. Exhaustion began to take over her bones, her hands tingling with numbness as she slowly began to relax. She was safe for now, but for how long?

"So, what's your name?" the other woman asked. Opening her eyes, she watched as the woman lay the infant in the bassinet next to her bed.

"Five."

"Five what?"

The other woman lifted the covers from her feet and began to explore the soles, making her wince in pain.

"Your name is Five?" She asked, pressing onto the sensitive skin. "Sorry, you have some infected cuts and blisters on your feet. I had to treat them last night. You definitely need to stay off of them for a little while so they can heal. So, your name is Five?"

Nodding, she winced again as the lady pressed on another sore. "We were named the age he took us. I'm Five."

Eyes widening at her confession, Five's face began to heat in embarrassment. She tried to sink into the bed, hiding from the stare the other woman bore into her.

"Well, Five is not going to do, is it? What should I call you instead? Do you remember your name?"

Five shook her head. "I don't remember anything from before. All I know is him."

The other woman nodded her head and replaced the covers over her feet. She walked over to her side and gingerly sat on the mattress beside her.

"What should I call you? I'm not using Five. My name is Millie. I own the bar you drifted into a couple of nights ago."

Fidgeting a little, sitting beside her on the bed, she continued, "I need to check your stitches. When you collapsed, you were bleeding pretty bad from the birth, and I had to stitch up your perineum where you tore. We need to make sure they're not infected. I gave you an intravenous antibiotic in your IV, but I still need to check the wound."

Five looked around the room, and her gaze landed back on Millie's dark brown eyes. "Are you a doctor or something?"

Smiling, Millie shook her head. "Or something. I have a lot of medical knowledge and first aid experience, but the only thing I'm a doctor at is slinging drinks. Can I check your stitches?"

She nodded and turned away as Millie lifted the sheets above her knees. She stared at a poster on the wall as the other woman prodded at her, making her hiss in pain. The poster had the name John Denver and advertised a song about the Rocky Mountains.

"Denver," she said to the woman.

"Hmm?" She asked as she lifted her head above the sheet to look at her.

"Denver. I like the name Denver."

Millie smiled and looked over at the tattered poster hanging on the wall. "Denver it is. Do you have an idea for a last name?"

Nodding, she said, "Rhodes. I want to be Denver Rhodes."

"Denver Rhodes it is. Your stitches look good. Since you're awake and alert, I can remove your IV. Stay in bed and ask for help if you need to use the restroom. Your feet need to heal. The stitches look good, and your baby is healthy. Rest up, and I'll be up to check on you in a few minutes," Millie said as she stood up from the bed, covering her body back up with the thin sheet.

"Are you sure you're not a doctor?"

Millie smirked and shook her head. "Take care of that baby. I'll be back in a few minutes with a more substantial meal for you."

Denver watched as Millie turned the light down low and silently clicked the door shut behind h

Chapter 2

BREATHING DEEPLY BEHIND THE closed door, Millie shuddered at seeing that poor girl's body—blonde hair, matted with dirt, thin and brittle from a neglected life. Wide blue eyes, hazed over from years of abuse and fear. Scars littered her pale skin, and the puckered white memories of pain left forever on her had a tear leaking from her eye. She sniffled, wiped away the evidence of emotion, and locked down her heart. Millie knew that her world was changing as soon as that girl collapsed.

"Denver Rhodes," Millie said, shaking her head as she walked away from the spare bedroom. She needed to order some supplies for that new baby and ward. She needs more clothing. Flipping off the lights in the hallway of the large home, she walked downstairs, past the kitchen, and to the locked cold storage. Entering the code onto the pad, the steal door opened with a woosh, frigid air hitting her face, her body shivering with the temperature change.

The door closed behind her with a soft click, red lighting leading her toward the back of the large room. Her collection covered the shelves along the walls of the room.

"Hello, my babies." She whispered with a smile.

Chapter 3

Denver's eyes opened slowly, adjusting to the dark room. She heard whimpering beside her and looked at the baby in the bassinet. Smiling, she reached over for the infant and held her closely to her chest, humming a tune under her breath as she slowly traced the soft skin on her baby's cheek.

"What should I call you?" She whispered as the baby began to root her mouth closer to Denver's chest. Exhaling with a soft smile, she lowered the neck of her shirt and fed the baby her breast, wincing when she latched on with hunger. Denver looked around the sparse room, wondering when she would have to leave and what she would do when she did. Tears began to coat and dry her cheeks as she took in her situation. No matter where she goes or what she has to do, at least she is away from Mister and Daddy. She got her baby away from the Daddy.

She closed her eyes and rested, wincing as she shifted her weight on the bed and pain lanced across her lower stomach. Denver left that house of horrors in the middle of the night. Daddy brought home another daughter and named her Eight. She was so tiny and young. Blonde hair, a halo around her head, and dirt coated her baby cheeks. Denver's anger began to boil over as she was told to introduce Eight to the other girls and put her in the training room.

She had rubbed her swollen belly, wondering what would happen to her baby when she finally gave birth. Would he get rid of the infant, or would he have trained the baby too? Most of the girls didn't survive the training room, and looking at the little girl, Denver knew she wouldn't be one of them.

Late that night, Denver snuck down to that special room, hoping Mister wouldn't hear her clumsy feet as she stumbled down the hall. He was passed out cold in his bed, thanks to the whiskey he liked to drown in. She unlocked that door and escaped into the cold winter night with Eight on her heels. Once she got the little girl to a police station, telling her to run inside, she began her run for her life. Denver knew that Mister wouldn't let her live after her betrayal, or he would punish her in the most horrific way. And she received a lot of punishment from the Mister.

A sharp cry split the air and woke Denver from her own musings. She lifted the baby to her shoulder and began patting her as Millie did, giggling when a large belch escaped from the small mouth. She really needs to think of a name for the baby.

She moved the baby to the crook of her arm and lifted her head to smell her soft head, the silky fuzz tickling her nose. The baby looked a lot like a doll she used to have. Dolly.

"I'm going to name you Dolly." She whispered as the baby drifted back into a peaceful, innocent sleep. God help her; she hoped that her new baby could stay innocent.

The pain of giving birth to this miracle is an experience she could never forget in her lifetime. Even more painful than any of the disciplines Daddy gave her. She remembered walking along the highway late in the evening. The moon hid its glow amid the streetlamps that shone sporadically along the deserted highway.

The tightening pain she felt in her stomach and across her back had Denver collapsing to her knees, panting breaths fogging in the cold night. The first contraction, she screamed, unable to prevent the sound from escaping her body. The intensity of the agony was one that she had never experienced and one she hoped never to have again.

Denver managed to move herself off the highway and toward the dry gutter out of the way of sight. At her most vulnerable, she knew that she could not protect herself. On her hands and knees, she could feel the urge to push, like she felt when she had to go to the bathroom, and she screamed again as the overwhelming pressure took over the core of her body. She was going to die here tonight, and no one would find her rotting corpse for days, weeks, months. Wolves would steal her baby, which would be raised in the wild amongst the pack.

Denver laughed softly to herself at her fanatical worries while giving birth to this angel. Is that going to be her life now, creating nonsensical fantasies that may overtake her analytical mind in the name of motherly love? When she felt the relief of the baby expelling from her system, she was frozen to the ice-cold ground, unable to move for seconds that felt like hours. Then, a small, weak cry pierced the darkest night, echoing off the walls of the freezing sky. Denver immediately raised herself from the packed earth and picked up her new baby, cradling the little body to her own for warmth.

She tried her best to clean off the white gunk and bloody gore that covered the baby and wrapped it in the only spare shirt she had. When she discovered her pregnancy, Daddy gave her books on how to care for it, and

Denver knew what she had to do. She removed a shoestring from her tennis shoe and tied off the umbilical cord that was hanging low from the baby's body. That's one positive thing she could say about all her years with Mister. He let her read. She couldn't leave the house and was never allowed to watch television or any other entertainment. She wasn't stupid; Denver knew she wasn't supposed to be there and had a home somewhere else, but when you're chained to a bed, what other choice do you have in your life? She began to nag him into either bringing her something to do or killing her. Somedays, she wished he would have just killed her.

Denver slowly moved her new baby over to the bassinet, the soft snores bringing a smile to her face. She's glad that Daddy never killed her. The overwhelming love she feels for this itty bitty creature is an emotion she doesn't even know how to describe. How could something that gave her so much turmoil, so much pain and suffering be able to produce such a love that the need to protect her and love her overcomes all other necessities? Such a love that Denver has never experienced for herself. Not with Mister or Daddy, anyway.

Chapter 4

Denver slept the sleep of the dead, so drained she was. Bone-deep exhaustion filled her pores; her bones felt so brittle she could shatter with the least amount of pressure, mentally and physically. The only reason she had to actually live was lying next to her. Her little Dolly. Pain filled her entire body, from her head to her feet, and she couldn't move without the lightning coursing through her veins, having her hiss with agony.

It's been barely a few days since she arrived in this little town. Millie has been taking such good care of her, bringing her food and helping her with Dolly. But it's time for her to start moving around. She could feel her muscles begin to clamp up with tightness. Her own body betrayed her with the loss of strength. Denver doesn't remember ever being so weak, not even with punishments from Daddy.

A knock on the door had her lifting her head as Millie came in with another tray of food. The smell of the chicken soup warred with the sweat floral perfume that drifted up to her own nose and permeated the area of her room.

"Oh, honey. You look so flushed. What's wrong?" Millie said as she lowered the tray to the side table and rushed over to her side, feeling Denver's forehead with the back of her hand.

"Oh, you have a fever. Sweet baby." Denver watched as the other woman began to rush around the small room, gathering supplies. She opened her eyes again when she felt a cool towel brush across her face. A haze covered her vision. Millie looked like an angel as the woman wiped a fevered sweat from her clammy skin.

Visions of Denver's recent past colored her sight as she began to drift into a dream. Memories of Daddy caning her and raping her. Residual burn pains from her torture had her screaming, struggling to get away from Mister.

She can't survive this again. Denver will die before she ever goes through this again.

Chapter 5

Filling the syringe with an antibiotic for the young woman on the bed, Millie shook her head in anger. No young woman should ever have to be in this condition. Whoever hurt this beautiful girl deserves to die a painful death.

Millie placed the needle of the syringe into the port of Denver's IV, injecting another dose of medication before placing the cap back onto the needle. She put the syringe back into the pocket of her apron. Walking back to the bathroom, Millie pulled a washrag from the shelf and soaked it in cold tap water, wringing it out and walking back to her charge. She softly bathed Denver's sweaty brow and face, tucking the cold cloth behind Denver's neck before checking on the baby.

Bright blue eyes shone up at her from the bassinet, and she picked up the baby and cradled it in her arms.

"Looks like you need another diaper change, little one." She said, wrinkling her nose at the smell. Millie never had the chance to be a mother, nor did she ever desire children. Still, after reading up on the internet and continued practice with the baby, she feels much more comfortable alone with the infant.

She changed the diaper and deposited the dirty diaper into the new genie trash she recently purchased. She had to shop for quite a few extra items that she never had to buy before Denver drifted into her life. Millie carried the baby toward the kitchen and began to make a bottle of formula. She knew that Denver wanted to nurse, but with her being out for several days because of this fever, there was only one way to feed the baby.

A muffled breaking sound distracted Millie from her chore, and she looked toward the side of the house where she had heard the noise. Walking toward the sound, she stopped when the baby began to cry in angry hunger.

"And my pipes are empty, so you will have to deal with the substitute, little one." She snickered at the screaming baby, offering the bottle's nipple to the hungry infant.

"Dolly, gotta remember, she wanted to call you Dolly," Millie said to herself. The baby finished the bottle, and Millie placed it into the sink before patting Dolly's back, giggling at a loud burp.

"You sure burp like a man." She said as she rubbed Dolly's back. Millie turned to take the baby back to her momma, stopping when she saw Denver standing in the kitchen way. She swayed unbalanced, one hand holding herself up on the wall. Her eyes were glazed over from the fever, the white nightdress sticking to her body from the sweat that coated her skin. She wavered uneasily, staring at Millie and Dolly, her blonde hair matted from the fevered sweat.

"Denver, what are you doing out of bed?"

Millie's eyes widened when she saw a sharp piece of glass in Denver's right hand.

"I'm not going back. I refuse to go back. I will die before you bring me to him." Denver yelled, bringing the clear glass up to her neck and pressing into the soft skin above her jugular.

"No!" Millie screamed, rushing toward the young woman.

Chapter 6

OPENING HER EYES, LIGHT poured into her sight, making her groan in pain as the feeling of knives pierced her eyes. Pain has been her only companion lately as she took stock of all her aches and pains. Gingerly sitting up, she groaned at the tightness of her neck and reached up to wince at the bandage and new wound at her neck. Denver didn't remember how she received it or when. Slowly looking over, she smiled at the awake bundle looking up from the bassinet.

Denver's breasts were incredibly swollen and sore, milk leaking and soaking her shirt. She reached over for Dolly and brought the infant to her chest, worry coloring her vision as the baby fought to take the breast. Finally, Dolly latched and began to suckle, and Denver sighed with a breath of relief. She lay back against the headboard and closed her eyes as relief left her, the feeling of stinging suction at her breast a new comfort.

A knock at the door preceded Millie's opening, and she walked into her room with a tray of food.

"You seem to have some kind of sense of when I'm awake and hungry," Denver said with a smile as she switched Dolly from the now empty breast to her other full one.

"Oh good, she's still nursing. I was worried that she wouldn't want to after the last couple of days." Millie said as she set the tray of food down on the nightstand.

"I don't understand. What do you mean?"

"You were sick. You had an infection, and your fever was incredibly high. You couldn't nurse; you were delirious, and so I had to feed Dolly with formula until you recovered. I do need to ask, child. What the fuck!"

Denver jumped at the anger flashing in the older woman's dark brown eyes. Dolly began to cry, and Denver lifted the baby to burb her.

"I'll help burp the baby. You start at the beginning and tell me everything. I was feeding Dolly, and you, in your fevered, delirious state, broke a window and tried to slice your own neck with a shard of glass. So, I will ask again. What the fuck. Start at the beginning and leave nothing out. I need to know what you brought to my house and what I need to do to protect you and this baby!"

Denver looked down at her lap and took a deep breath, grasping the sheets in her hands with anxiety. She took a deep breath.

"He took me when I was five years old. I don't remember my parents or my life from before. Sometimes, I get snippets of a beautiful blonde woman hugging me, but I don't know if that was my mother or dreams of what I might have had.

The man who took me forced me to call him Mister. If I didn't, I received discipline.

Sometimes a whipping with a belt or a can, sometimes a beating with a fist."

Denver watched as Millie carried the now-sleeping baby to the bassinet to lay her down to sleep. She watched as the older woman sat next to her on the bed and handed her the plate of food, the smell of toasted bread and cheese making her a little nauseous.

"Go on," Millie said.

Denver took a bite of the buttered toast and chewed slowly, trying to create the strength to finish the story.

"I was with Mister for 13 years. I was 10 when he first raped me. I didn't understand, of course, but he said that it was what we were supposed to do, so I didn't question it... at first."

Denver took another bite of bread and reached for the glass of juice next to her, taking a long sip and wrinkling her nose at the sweetness.

"It wasn't until I turned 13, I think, that I realized what he was doing was so wrong. Even though he kidnapped me and beat me, he still supplied me with plenty of books and educational tools. I think I'm pretty smart for a girl with a kindergarten-level education. If I had to thank him for anything, it would have been education because of my boredom and curiosity." Denver chuckled, giving up on the toast that felt like ash in her mouth.

"He brought home another girl and named her Eight. He raped her that night, and she fought. She screamed so loud that I thought the neighbors would investigate. But no one came, and soon Eight became part of our 'family.' Then Ten joined soon after. As I grew older, I became less of one of his girls and more of the caretaker. He would beat and rape me to keep the other girls in line."

Denver sat the plate on the table next to her and sat up to stretch. She sat back against the bed frame and covered her lap with the sheet, watching as Millie stared at her with shock in her eyes.

"Then he figured out how to make money. He would sell me for the night to other men. I would still have to care for the other girls, clean, and handle his physical anger, but then go to other men at night. I think I would have preferred it if Mister had used me compared to the others he sold me to. One man would put out cigarettes on my skin while he raped me. Another choked me until I passed out. Mister's only rule was to keep me alive to care for his girls during the day.

It was when I became pregnant that the abuse and rapes stopped. Mister started to become loving to me again, talking about how he could make money by selling a new daughter. He still raped me, but I didn't fight, he didn't hurt me, and life was becoming easier."

Denver watched as Millie wiped a tear from her eye and pulled her knees up to her chest.

"One of my rapists found out I was pregnant when he tried to buy me again for another night. He demanded that Mister handed me over and offered him a lot of money, more than any of us had ever seen. I knew that Mister was considering it, and I was scared. But he told me that I was his precious girl and he would never get rid of me, and I believed him until he brought home another little girl. He named her Five, and she was his newest girl. I knew then he replaced me, and as soon as my baby was born, he was going to sell me to that evil man. The man made us call him Daddy.

That night, I broke into Five's room, helped her out of the house, and we walked together to the closest police station. I left her there for them to find her parents, and I began walking away from everything as quickly as possible. I left behind the other two girls. I didn't want to, but I had to think about me and my baby. I knew that I would have the baby very soon. I left promising that as soon as my baby and I were safe, I was going to send someone to rescue them. I began walking without any thought or knowledge of where I would end up."

Millie stood up and brushed tears from her cheeks. "How long were you walking for?" She asked.

Denver looked into her face and whispered, "Two full days of walking, not including the hours of labor for Dolly. I estimate about two days of walking."

She watched Millie pace around the room. "Do you know what city you walked from?" Millie asked.

Denver nodded. "Richmond."

"Do you think you could find the house?"

Nodding again, Denver answered, "I know the address. He used to make me address his bills."

Chapter 7

THE GLOOM OF THE darkness was an irony to the fireworks exploding inside Millie's chest. The plan of a hunt, the perfect execution of a plan, and her trophies were the combination of precision filling her body and giving her a high. She pulled up to an older home located in a newer neighborhood. Richmond, Texas. A smaller city that seems to be an idyllic home for families to raise children. Evil finds its way into the most unassuming places, it seems. After all, look at her.

Driving past the house where her prey was hiding, unaware of her hunt, Millie parked in an empty driveway, shutting down her van and covering her long dark hair with a black beanie. Excitement filled her veins, leaking from her pores with every moment that passed as she prepared. Millie climbed out of the van and gently closed the driver's side door, hoping the absence of light wouldn't expose her to the neighborhood. She opened the back door, pulled the large duffle bag toward her, opened the zipper, and double-checked her supplies, lovingly stroking her favorite sharpened cleaver, the streetlight reflecting off the cold, hard steel.

She stroked the blade, feeling her face tighten with the smile that curved across her face. Zipping her bag closed, Millie began to walk toward her prey's home, shivering as the cold winter wind battered her face. Twinkling Christmas lights scattered green and red, the reflection in the darkened windows shattering as her reflection passed each home.

The house that held her prey was dark, eerie shadows heralding her incoming evil as she walked up to the front door, twisting the doorknob and walking in like she belonged. Millie learned long ago that the more she tried to sneak around, the more suspicious she looked.

Walking into a situation as if you belonged, fewer people were likely to notice you.

She silently closed the door behind her and locked the deadbolt, something her prey should have done, although a simple lock wouldn't have kept her from her mission this cold evening. The house looked ordinary, almost bland in its dark, evil glory. Millie slowly walked toward the back of the house, keeping alert for any sounds that may herald her prey, becoming alarmed about her hunt. Murmurs of cries and moans echo as she finds stairs leading to a lower house level. Harsh, hushed whispers cover the sounds of her footsteps with every movement down the old stairs.

She pulled a syringe from her bag as she reached the bottom of the staircase and took in the scenery around her. She definitely found the torture chamber of the evil that was housed in this city. Chains attached to the brick walls hung limply, black dried blood splattered onto the floor, flaking with old age. Two young women hung from chains at the end of the brick wall, their bodies abused and beaten, blood leaking from every orifice, bellies distended with obvious pregnancies.

Both girls were gagged, and their eyes widened with fear as she crept closer to their bounded forms. Millie held a finger to her lips, mimicking a shush as she slid her body into a darkened corner to wait. She knew how to wait for her prey and silently anticipate the moment she could pounce as if she were a lion to a gazelle. However, she's hunting a hyena, a worthless scavenger not worthy of life, not an innocent lamb.

Waiting quietly in the dark, the creaking of the stairs alerts Millie to his arrival. Denver's Mister. She waits patiently as he taunts the two young girls.

"Are you going to tell me where Five is?" He asks quietly, tracing a knife around her bare skin. Millie watches her cry as the girl denies any knowledge of the young woman that Millie found on her own doorstep.

"Mister, I told you. We don't know. She wasn't here when we woke up. We don't know anything."

Tears track down the teenager's face as Millie watches the other teenager grit her teeth when the Mister turns towards her.

"And you? My dear Eight. Where is my girl? Where is Five?"

Millie began to creep closer as she felt the tension escalate with the teenager. As she walked closer to the monster, her footsteps silent under the cracked concrete and the smell of coppery blood pungent in the stale air, she stood as tall as she could, ready to plunge the needle into his skin.

"I don't know anything about Five, and even if I did, I wouldn't tell you, pig!" Eight screams, her chains rattling in the quiet basement. Millie lifted the syringe and struck just as the teenager spit into his face, the perfect distraction for her to inject the paralytic into the monster.

Watching as he slapped his neck, his eyes glazing over before dropping to the hard concrete with a thud, his head cracking on the hard floor. She watched with a pleasurable shiver as blood began to pool from underneath his head.

Looking up at the two girls, she asked, "I have some business to take care of. Do you have somewhere to go when I release you?"

Eight shook her head, her blue eyes wide with fear. "I don't even know where I am. Even if I did, I was an orphan before he found me. Who are you? Do you know where Five is?"

Millie nodded her head as she searched the body for a set of keys to the handcuffs chaining the girls to the wall.

"You know Five, don't you?" The second girl, Eleven, cried. "Please take us to her. Please."

Millie stared for a moment at the two young girls, broken, bleeding, and heavily pregnant. *God dang you, Denver, for setting me on this course!* She thought to herself as she unlocked Eight's chain. She stared at the two teenagers, both blonde and blue-eyed copies of one another. They look like they could be sisters to Denver waiting back at her home.

"I know Five. She calls herself Denver and gave birth to a beautiful little girl." Millie heaved a sigh. "Yes, you can come with me. Go upstairs and pack whatever you need. Clean yourselves up as best as you can. I have a little something I need to do, so wait near the front door for me."

Millie unlocked the second set of handcuffs and winced as the two girls stood before her, rubbing their bloody wrists. She watched with a burgeoning anger and madness toward the evil man lying on the floor. Millie grabbed his arms and pulled his heavy body toward the ankle manacles attached to the wall. She locked the cuffs around his wrists before returning to her bag to retrieve her tools. Pulling out a jar of formaldehyde and her favorite bone saw, she walked back toward the body that was now trying to struggle on the floor. He seems to be trying to wake up.

"Oh, Mister. You're awake. You had some fun with those girls; now it's my turn to have fun with you." Millie sang, crouching on the floor next to him.

"That shot was a paralytic, but I promise you will still feel everything, My dear Mister. And I'm afraid I'm going to love this a bit more than you."

Millie began to saw at his wrist, hitting the bone and working the saw hard to cut through. She smiled at his screams as they pierced the silent basement, licking at the blood that spattered across her face.

"Oh yes, I do love this more."

Chapter 8

THE VAN PULLED UP to the home behind her bar. They finally arrived back home. After collecting the new piece for her collection, removing as much evidence as possible of the three girls living in the home took several hours.

Eleven and Eight even boxed up some of Denver's belongings and books that she had collected over the years. They walked up toward the door, the teen girls holding onto one another for support. The front door ripped open, and Denver stood before her, holding Dolly, a shocked, surprised look on her face. Millie chuckled as the girls squealed and began to hug each other.

Millie stepped past the girls and into the house. "Come on, ladies, bring it inside. Denver set up a tray of food and juices for your friends.

I need to call a doctor, and we need to get some sleep sometime tonight. I have a bar to run.

Denver turned toward Millie. "What? No doctors. Please. They'll just take us away. I don't want them to take us away."

Shaking her head, Millie shushed the shaking girl. "No one is going to take any of you away. The doctor is my friend and my personal confidant. She won't say anything to anyone. But your friends are extremely abused and heavily pregnant. They need more medical attention than I can provide."

Millie began to walk away before turning back toward them. "Get some food in them, set them up in a room, and I'll be up soon with the doctor."

"Yes, Ma'am." They chorused as Millie nodded and walked toward her cold storage. "Ma'am." She liked the sound of that.

The cold storage door opened with a "whoosh" and a blast of cool air hitting Millie's face as she stepped over the threshold. She unpacked her tools on the steel table, reminding herself to clean and bleach them later. Removing the now full jar from the bag, she placed it on a shelf with reverence, staring at her growing collection. Jars filled the shelves, and Millie knew that she would need to put together another shelf as her collection grew.

Hearing footsteps behind her, she turned quickly, letting out a relieved breath as she saw her good friend, Amy. The lovely doctor walked right up to Millie, embracing her in a hug and a long kiss, their tongues dueling for a moment before Millie pulled back.

She lightly traced Amy's face with her fingers, her dark brown eyes sparkling with the reflection of the fluorescent lights swinging from the ceiling. Dark brown braided hair hung down Amy's back when the younger woman turned to help Millie unpack her bag.

"Did the new syringe work?" Amy asked as she handed the now empty bag to Millie.

"It did." Answered Millie, folding the bag and placing it on a shelf. "It was the best paralytic yet. If you come across any more, let me know. I enjoyed the quickness and longevity of the effects."

"I also may have brought back a few girls. They refused to let me leave them behind and wanted me to bring them to Denver."

Amy chuckled as she washed her hands in the sink. Millie held the door open for Amy and closed the cold storage door with a silent snick, locking the door behind her and following Amy into the kitchen. She began to pull out the fixings for sandwiches so she could feed the girls when screaming began to echo throughout the large house. Amy dropped the plates onto the counter and ran toward the staircase, Millie following her.

The vision from the doorway stopped Millie in her tracks as she stared at the young screaming girl being held down on the bed.

Blood poured out from between her legs, soaking the mattress as the young girl screamed and kicked her legs out in obvious pain.

"She's hemorrhaging. Losing the baby." Screamed Amy, startling Millie from her frozen spot in the doorway. She rushed over to where Denver stood, holding the thrashing girl to the bed, and grabbed a leg to prevent her from kicking the doctor.

"You!" Amy yelled at the scared girl on the other side of the room. "Grab her other leg and hold her down. I need to stop the bleeding. I can't save the baby, but I might be able to save her." Amy pointed to Denver. "You, run back downstairs and grab my bag and a bunch of towels. Fast." Millie watched the young woman rush out of the room and held the young girl tightly as Amy got to work to save her. A baby's scream pierced the air along with the moaning and crying of their patient. She knew it was going to be a long night.

Chapter 9

LAYING IN THE BED, Denver softly stroked the baby's cheek as she nursed, hungrily feeding after such a long night. They've only been here for less than a week, and Denver already feels so much safer than she has ever felt in her entire life. She heard a snore behind her and turned her head toward her younger bedmate. Eleven slept soundly behind her. She could feel a slight kicking from her sister's pregnant stomach dig into Denver's back.

Finished nursing, the baby in Denver's arms began to squirm with discomfort, so she sat up, rubbing and patting the baby's back to help her burp, just like Millie showed her. Smiling at the little belch, Denver laid the baby down at the end of the bed and began to change the dirty diaper, wrinkling her nose at the overwhelming smell permeating the room.

"How can such a little baby cause such a huge stink?" the small voice from the bed had Denver jerk in alarm.

"I tried not to wake you," Denver said as she finished diapering her daughter and cradling her in her arms.

Eleven shook her head. "It's fine. It's been a while since I actually slept in a bed. I'm not sure I would have gotten much more sleep anyhow." Denver watched as she sat up and stretched her arms up over her head. "Where are we?" Eleven asked.

"Safe," Denver said softly. "We're safe."

"Do you want to hold the baby? I named her Dolly because she reminds me of a little Doll."

Denver smiled when her sister nodded and laid the baby into the young girl's arms.

"Careful, watch the head." She said.

Eleven's eyes widened. "Why? Does it fall off or something?"

Denver shook her head and giggled a little. "Just support the head. That's what Millie taught me. I'm learning as I go along. Did you think of another name to use? Or can you go back to your old name from before Mister took us? I don't want to keep calling you what the monster named us."

"I remember the name Sarah. I don't know if it was mine or someone else's, but I really like the name Sarah."

Denver reached out and rubbed the young girl's blonde hair between her fingers. She wrinkled her nose at the grime and blood left behind on her fingertips. "Then Sarah, you will be. This is going to be a different life for us. A better life for us. I can feel it. The freedom. Can you?"

She watched as her sister traced a loving fingertip over the baby's soft face. "Do you think my baby will be as sweet as this? Do you think something as evil as Mister could give us something as beautiful and innocent as this baby?" She shook her head.

"I don't know how I feel right now. I am bloodied and bruised. My whole body hurts, and I watched the girl I think of as a sister nearly die last night. All that blood." Denver shivered with the memory.

She removed her baby from Sarah's arms. "Well, let's take it one step at a time—first, a hot shower. Then, real food. Come on, I'll show you how to use the shower." Denver walked away from the bed and turned her head when she noticed Sarah not following her.

"Is this a trick? Mister always played these tricks. I follow you, and he's in the next room, ready to punish me."

Denver shook her head. "You never have to worry about him again. We're safe from him, forever."

She watched as Sarah's eyes widened. "What about Daddy?" she whispered as she rubbed her pregnant belly.

Denver nodded. "I will talk to Ms. Millie. Tell her about Daddy. But right now, he doesn't know where we are or who rescued us; he has nothing. And Ms. Millie will protect us."

Sarah stood up quickly, her body wavering and raised a hand to her head. "How do you know she will protect us? You don't know her. You've only been here for a few days, only been gone for a week. How do you know she will protect us? No one can protect us from the Daddy!" She cried out with fear.

"I will protect you all. I brought you here, and I will keep you safe." Millie interrupted from the doorway. Denver jumped and turned toward the older woman.

"You need a bath, my dear. And some good food. Denver, show her where the shower is, and then come help me with some breakfast for the girls and Dr. Amy. Your young friend is going to be okay, but we couldn't save the baby. She's resting right now."

Millie turned to leave the room but looked back at Denver. "Oh, and did you tell her to use a different name than that God-awful number?"

"Yes, ma'am," Denver replied. "She chose the name Sarah. She doesn't remember if it's her name or not, but it's one she liked."

Millie nodded. "Good, I like it. Better than Denver, in my opinion. Now, show her the shower, and then come into the kitchen and tell me all about this Daddy you two are so scared of."

Nodding, Denver murmured, "Yes, ma'am." And waited for the bedroom door to shut before turning back toward her sister.

"Shower, food, info." She said as she walked into the bathroom, expecting Sarah to follow behind her.

Chapter 10

Walking into the kitchen, Millie stopped short at seeing Amy at the table nursing a whiskey in a shot glass. She washed her hands at the sink. Walking over to the table, Millie pulled out a chair and sat down, swiping the shot glass and taking her own sip.

"Well, whatcha thinking?" Millie asked as she refilled the glass with the whiskey and sipped at the strong liquor.

Amy shook her head and rubbed her hands over her face. "The evidence of abuse on those girls makes me so angry. Not only the fresh injuries but the old ones, too. The little one, I estimate to be only twelve years old, has several old breaks in her hands and feet that haven't healed right. I don't know what to think."

Millie filled the shot glass with more whiskey and handed it to Amy, watching as she swigged the drink.

"Please tell me you gutted him slowly. Made him feel every inch of abuse that he did to those little girls. I'm physically ill. And they're pregnant! I don't think any of them are over eighteen. Millie, what are we going to do? None of them have any IDs; they refuse any kind of medical help. Millie, they're so traumatized and scared. I don't know what to do!" Tears filled Amy's eyes.

Amy slammed the glass down onto the table, and the loud crack made Millie jump in her seat. Shaking her head, Millie removed the glass from Amy and stood up. "It's not over. I overheard the girls talking about someone else that hurt them repeatedly."

Walking over to the sink, Millie rinsed out the glass and placed it on the counter. She turned around and walked back toward the table.

"You took my glass," Amy said as she swigged whiskey straight from the bottle, wrinkling her nose at the burn and belched. Millie shook her head and took away the bottle from her friend. "You need to keep your wits about you. Let's get information from the girls, and then we can go hunting."

Amy shook her head. "What are you going to do with these girls?"

Shrugging her shoulders, Millie took a sip from the whiskey bottle. "Keep them, I suppose. I can't kick them out into the cold; I'm not calling the police here." She motioned toward the cold storage with her head. "The girls don't even remember who they are."

Standing up, Amy began to pace around the kitchen. "They're not stray dogs. You can't just keep them because you want to. And what about us? What I want. We both said we didn't want children. We got together."

"But we don't want to go."

Millie stood up sharply at the voice that interrupted their conversation. She looked over to the two young women standing in the kitchen entryway. Denver stood still, holding on to her younger companion. Both girls were too thin, and their eyes sunken.

"Shit, they look like they could be sisters, even twins," Amy said, sitting back at the table.

Millie pointed toward the chairs and invited the girls to sit. "If you're ready to talk, I'm here to listen. I won't ask you to leave, and I'm not calling the police or anything. No matter what you or anyone says, you'll have a home here with me." Millie shook her head slightly when Amy turned to give her a disappointed look.

Millie watched Denver look at the younger girl and sighed a relieved breath as the little girl nodded her head.

Denver clasped her hands together on the table. "I have been with Mister for so long, I have lost time. He named us the age we were when we took us. I estimate maybe I'm 17 or 18, but I can't be sure."

Amy stood up from the table, walked over to the refrigerator, pulled out two cold water bottles, returned to the table, and handed them to the girls. Denver nodded her thanks and took a drink.

"He brought home Eleven next. Then soon after, Eight. He demanded that we call him Mister, but we never knew any other name to call him. We were treated kind of decently well until we got our periods. That's when everything changed." Denver took another sip of the water, the audible gulp the prelude to her story Millie knew she wasn't going to like.

"Dolly isn't my first child. Mister had a partner who demanded that we call him Daddy. This is one of the men who forced us and made us pregnant. Then, he would come to take the baby and sell it. Dolly is my third baby."

Amy stood up and rushed to the sink, retching and throwing up. Millie sat in her chair in shock as she stared at the two young women.

Denver took another drink of water. "This is Eleven's and Eight's first pregnancy. There were also more than the three of us in the house. Once the girls got too old, they disappeared. Or if they never got pregnant or if they were too much trouble, they disappeared. I think they were sold to someone in Houston. My job was to care for the girls, but I knew I was getting too old when Mister began to pay less attention to me and more to the other two younger girls."

Sarah, sitting next to Denver, began to cry. Millie watched as the two girls hugged one another in comfort.

Millie leaned forward on the table, steepling her fingers together. "Did you witness anyone else come into the house? Were there other men? I need any and all information you can give us."

Denver shook her head. "No. I think it was just the two of them in that house. I really don't remember much. Mister would take us to other men who bought our services. I learned later on that they sold the babies, but I don't know to whom. Or if the people they sold the babies to even knew where the babies came from. I don't even know if Daddy knows we are gone yet. With all three of us pregnant at the same time, he hasn't been around in a while."

Amy walked back over and sat at the table after rinsing her mouth out at the sink. She shook her head. "Well, I helped the little one upstairs as much as possible here at the house, but with you refusing to go to the hospital, we can only pray that she doesn't develop an infection. I would like to examine you both and treat any injuries you may have. Especially you, Denver. With you just having a baby and with no prenatal care, I need to make sure that you are on your way to recovery."

The young blonde next to Denver cleared her throat. Millie and Amy both looked at her. "I don't want this baby." She said with a sob. Denver wrapped her arms around the young girl. "Can you do something about it? All I can think about is that horrible man on top of me. Hurting me, tearing me. I can't have this baby and know that the evil he put inside me is still inside me."

She sobbed against Denver's shoulder. "Shh, Sarah," Denver whispered against her hair. Millie locked eyes with Denver.

"How far along is she?" Millie asked.

Denver shrugged her shoulders. "Best estimate, about five months. I think she looks so much bigger than she is because she's so little, so young."

Amy looked at the young girl. "Are you sure this is what you want?"

Sarah nodded. "Yes. Absolutely."

Amy stood up from the table. I'll visit the lab to get everything I need. I need her comfortable. Make sure she eats a good meal tonight, and I'll be back tomorrow morning."

Amy leaned down, gave Millie a quick kiss on her lips, and walked out of the kitchen.

Millie looked at the two girls. "Well, you heard her. You need a good meal. How do tacos sound?" She asked as she stood up and began to gather ingredients

Chapter 11

SEVERAL DAYS LATER

Denver and Sarah lay together with their other "sister" in a large, soft bed. This was the softest bed she had ever been on before in her life, and she snuggled deep into the cushioned mattress. The drip of the faucet was overly loud in the silent bedroom. Her sister has been out of it while fighting an infection since their rescue and the miscarriage of her baby. Sarah has been mostly silent and morose since her decision to end her pregnancy. Denver felt as if the world was falling apart and she might be losing her sisters. They were the only family she had, other than Dolly, and she didn't want to let them go.

They were all teenagers, forced into adulthood too early. She overheard the conversations between Millie and Amy in the kitchen the other day. Words like trauma and therapy. Then, she overheard the word revenge. She sat up in bed and walked over toward the bassinet to check on her sleeping Dolly. The baby has been especially quiet lately and not wanting to feed as often. She didn't cry anymore, either. Her breasts were feeling overly full, and she knew she would need to express a little. But first, she needed to stretch her legs and get herself a snack. Maybe bring a small snack for her sisters.

Her bare feet padded quietly on the floor, the cold seeping into her skin as she walked silently into the kitchen. The darkness through the window didn't give her an estimate of what time it was exactly, but she knew it was late in the evening with how silent the house was. She could hear the neighbor's animals settling down, the snicker of the horses, and the squeal of the pigs, declaring their need for dinner. Millie had to go into the bar to work, and Dr. Amy was at the hospital. They woke her before they left and asked her to keep an eye on the girls as if she needed to be asked.

As she walked into the kitchen, she turned to see the cold storage door. It was always locked, and she was a little curious about why a cold storage room would be locked up so tight. What could Millie keep in there that would need to be behind lock and key?

Tonight, though, Millie must have been in a hurry because of the emergency at the bar. The door was cracked open as if it wasn't shut all the way. Denver looked around the room, half expecting someone to jump out and stop her as she slowly opened the door to the cold storage room. The darkness of the room rivaled the pitch blackness outside, and she felt along the wall for a light switch that would light up the room.

Feeling the switch, she flicked it up and blinked her eyes, trying to focus with the bright light blinding her vision. The room was filled with shelves. Next to her was a large industrial stainless steel sink. A strong smell was overpowering her senses, as if the room was filled with open pickle jars. She coughed and wrinkled her nose, pulling her shirt over her face to hide from the odor.

Looking around the room, she stepped farther in and began to examine the items on the shelves. Large jars and small jars covered the shelving, each with a placard in front of the shelf detailing a name and an action.

Picking up one jar, Denver squealed, quickly placing it back on the shelf and backing away toward the door. Preserved eyeballs stared back at her accusingly. She began to breathe heavily, clutching her chest as she felt a tightening across her diaphragm. Walking back toward the shelf, she picked up the small placard and read,

"Jonathon, watching girls change, purveyor of child porn."

The jar next on the shelf held a jar with a preserved tongue, a placard that read, "Eric, Liar. Bears false witness in court."

She picked up the placard and stared at the words before her. They began to blur as her eyes teared up. What did she stumble into?

The door shut with a soft snick behind her, and Denver jumped, turning around in alarm at the sight of Millie standing in the doorway. Millie walked toward her, picked up the placard from the floor, and quietly set it back on the shelf.

"He told lies in court about a young girl that was raped. He provided a fake alibi against her rapist, which caused him to get acquitted. He needed to pay for his crimes. I also have the rapist around here, too, if you want to see it."

Denver began to back away from Millie and toward the closed door. "What is this? Who are you?" She asked, shaking her head with confusion.

Denver backed away more as Millie turned and walked toward her and the door. "We should get out of this room. The fumes can get to you if you're in here too long and not used to it." She opened the door and waited for Denver to walk through, shutting it behind them and locking it. They were standing in the empty kitchen. Denver watched as Millie walked over toward the freezer and pulled out a whiskey bottle, pouring herself a glass before joining her at the table.

"I'd offer you a glass, but you're a bit underaged and nursing, so…"

Denver fearfully laughed as she glanced toward the locked, cold storage door. "You're worried about laws? What I just saw doesn't seem you cared too much about laws."

Millie took a sip of the cold whiskey before she answered. "I care very much about laws. Every single one of those trophies belonged to someone who broke those laws and tried to get away from it. I make society safe from monsters by being a bigger monster."

"Does Dr. Amy know about this? So many jars, so many shelves." Denver said, shaking her head.

"Amy helped me with my first one. She has taught me how to remove my trophies with optimum precision. She brings me drugs that help keep the sinners still so I can work quickly. In some cases, she helps me destroy evidence. Amy is my other half, my lover. Amy was the first victim and my first restitution. But that's not my story to tell."

Millie finished off her glass of whiskey and refilled it, taking another sip. "When I say the monster that has held you captive all your life will never bug you again, I mean it. He is now a trophy on my shelf. When you give me all the information you can on this 'Daddy,' he will also be placed on my shelf. The question I have for you is, what are you going to do about this?"

"What am I supposed to do?" Denver asked as she rubbed her hands over her face. "I am a nobody. I don't even know who I am or where I belong. You've done more for me than anyone had my entire life, and I've only been here for a week, I think. Maybe 2. Who am I to know right from wrong? Evil from good. You did to them what I've wanted to do to Mister for years: take him apart piece by piece."

Millie nodded and finished her glass. She stood up and walked to the sink, rinsing out the glass. Denver stared at Millie's back, standing up from her chair, when she heard a shuffle from her bedroom.

"Go take care of your sisters. We'll talk more later. Don't tell anyone what you saw today, especially the other two. They need to heal more, mentally and physically."

Nodding, Denver walked out of the kitchen, her mind wheeling from everything she learned.

Denver walked back into her room, staring at the two young girls holding one another on the bed. They were finally safe, but what did she bring them into? Denver hoped she didn't pull them out of the stove just to throw them in the fire.

Taking a deep breath, Denver walked over to the bassinet and leaned over to check on her baby. She stared at the beautiful little girl lying so still in the bed as if she was a little doll—her little Dolly.

Her little Dolly wasn't moving.

Denver reached down to wake up the baby, placing her hand on the chest. Her baby's lips were bluish, with dark blue veins highlighted in her tiny, pale face. Dolly's chest wasn't moving. She wasn't breathing. Denver stood over her precious baby, unsure of what was happening until she realized that her Dolly wasn't alive. Her chest felt tight as she backed away from the bassinet. Tears began to pour down her face as she tried to catch her breath. Clasping her chest, she fell to her knees in the room; the thud of her body hitting the floor echoed. Both young girls sat up in bed as she turned and stared at them in horror.

Then Denver screamed.

Chapter 12

Days passed with Denver stuck in a fog. Life seemed to have little meaning as hours passed relentlessly. Her body feels too heavy to move. She lay in bed, unable to sleep yet unable to keep her eyes open. Staring at the sandwich that lay on the tray near the floor, Denver watches as the flies hover over the food that was supposed to nourish her. She can't even nourish her own child, a piece of her own body. Denver closed her eyes once more, welcoming the feel of sandpaper behind her eyelids.

Denver opened her eyes as the bed moved next to her. She rolled over and spotted her younger sister cuddling up next to her. Wrapping her arms around the young girl, Denver pulled her closer to her body and took a deep breath.

"What are you doing?" Denver asked.

"I miss you. I need you." The young girl cried.

Denver sniffed a little as her eyes welled up with tears. "I'm right here." She mumbled into the young girl's hair.

"No, you're not. You haven't been here for days. Sarah and Ms. Millie said you need to heal and to leave you be, but I need you. I picked a name."

Denver brushed the tangled blonde hair away from her sister's soft face. "Oh? What name is that?"

With a hiccup and a little sob, she said, "Bridget. Dr. Amy and Ms. Millie were watching a movie about a diary, and I heard the name Bridget Jones. I think it sounded nice, so that's going to be my name."

A little confused at the story, Denver nodded her head. "I think Bridget is a great name." Denver began to close her eyes again, the pain of dried tears she could barely feel over the pain in her heart drifting off into another deep sleep as she felt soft fingers stroke her face.

The room was enveloped in darkness, the bleak area of the room reflecting how she felt in her soul. Denver blinked her eyes open, rubbing the crusty sleep from her eyelids as she sat up in her bed. Her entire body ached with pain. She stood up shakily and looked around the dark room, willing her eyes to adjust to the everlasting pitch-blackness. Stumbling to the bathroom, she relieved herself and splashed water onto her face.

The entire house seemed quiet. She never understood the phrase, quiet as a tomb before now. Not even the creaking of the home disturbed the late-night silence. She looked around the room and sighed at the loss of the baby furniture that once sat near the side of her bed. The entire room seemed to have been cleared out while she slept. Denver jumped and covered her eyes as a soft light from the lamp behind her clicked on.

Turning around and blinking to clear her vision, Denver crumbled in tears at the sight of Ms. Millie and Dr. Amy standing at the door. Both women were in their silk pajamas, hanging softly on their thin bodies. Amy's head was covered with a dark silk bonnet, while Millie wore her hair in foam curlers.

"We thought it would be easier for you if we removed some of your things while you slept. Everything's in storage when you're ready to go through it." Amy said as Millie walked up to Denver and wrapped her arms around the grieving teen. Denver felt something unlock in her chest, like a release of emotions that erupted from her body as she cried into Millie's shoulder. The older woman's nightshirt became uncomfortably wet with Denver's tears as she sobbed.

Denver felt a hand touch the back of her hair and felt the heat from Amy's body behind her. Comfort from the two women wrapped around Denver's heart, and she collapsed between them, their healing love enveloping her. Denver closed her eyes and relaxed between the two women as they held her. She felt more bodies close in around her and looked up, surprised to see Sarah and Bridgete in their circle.

"We're here for you. You're not alone; we will always be here for you." Millie said as she kissed the top of Denver's head.

Denver turned around and looked at Amy. "Was it my fault? Did I not take good enough care of my Dolly? Did I kill her?"

Amy shook her head. "No, baby. She passed away from SIDS. Nothing you could have done. Likely because of the neglect and abuse you experienced, no prenatal care, and stress."

Blinking, Denver backed away from their circle and sat on her bed. "What's SIDS?"

Amy sat next to her on the bed. "SIDS is Sudden Infant Death Syndrome. Many variables can lead to a baby passing away from SIDS, but none of it is your fault. You did everything that you could. It isn't your fault."

Denver began to cry again and covered her face with her hands. She felt someone pull her hands away and looked at Bridgette kneeling on the floor beside the bed. Sarah stood behind her.

"We miss Dolly too. I wish we could have had her forever." Bridgette said, her bright blue eyes shiny with unshed tears. "But I missed you more. I need you. I can't do this without you."

Sarah sat next to Bridgette. "Me neither. I need you, too. You're like the mother we needed when we were with Mister. You kept us strong after Daddy visited. Now we need you even though we're free."

Denver nodded. "I want to hurt him so badly. I wish I could have hurt Mister the way he hurt us. I wish I could hurt Daddy. I want to make him feel as bad as I feel. I am so angry, so mad." She shook her head and screamed into her hands. "I want revenge!" She yelled.

Millie nodded. "Then we will get you your revenge."

Amy agreed. "It's time."

Chapter 13

THE HOUSE SAT IN the dark, empty and alone, as the women waited in the van watching the abandoned home. The world stayed asleep as the Millie and the three girls plotted their revenge.

"I'm scared. What if he comes in while we're in there." Bridgette cried as they began to climb out of the van.

"There are four of us and one of him," Mille said as she pulled her duffle bag out of the trunk of the van. "Besides, he may not even show up. This is mostly a fact-finding mission. There must be some kind of information on the men in this house. Let's stick together, and everything will be fine."

Mille quietly closed the van door and walked up to the home's front door, followed by the three young girls. She opened the unlocked front door and walked in, closing and locking the door behind Bridgette. Sarah and Denver led the way toward Mister's bedroom and office. As they passed the basement door, Bridgette began to cry harder. Millie looked toward the basement door, remembering her time with their jailer. The faint odor of sickly sweet death was still lingering. She smiled before focusing her attention on her youngest ward.

"I don't think I can do this," Bridgette whined.

Milled grasped Bridgette's hand and held on. "We're not going anywhere but the office. I promise. We won't be here long, but then we'll go. But you can do this. We can do this together. I promise I won't leave you." Mille said, staring at Bridgette until the young girl nodded.

They followed the other two into the office, and Millie shut the door behind them. "Okay, girls. Sarah, you're on look out. Keep your eyes on the window and let me know if any cars park out front. Bridgette, you can start searching the closet. All paperwork can be important, so save everything. I'll look through this file cabinet, Denver; you look through the desk. Let's get in and out as quickly as we can. We can use any information on any men who came through this house."

The girls nodded and mumbled, "Yes, ma'am." as they began to search the office. Mille pulled out one of the file shelves and began searching through the papers. "I'm looking for names, descriptions, anything that tells us who has come into this house. Everyone who knows what was happening to you is guilty. Denver, find a box or a bag, empty it out, and we can place any paperwork there to go through back at our house. Sarah, keep your eyes out. Any car is suspect. If they drive by slow or more than once, we pack up and leave."

Minutes seemed to drone on, feeling like hours, and Millie closed the last file drawer on the cabinet. They had several bags and boxes full of paperwork to go through. She was grateful that the monster who was in charge of this trafficking and baby-buying operation was incredibly meticulous with his records. He even kept a journal detailing the "adoption" process with prospective clients.

She laid another paper in a box with a lawyer's information. Millie was shocked at how many *respectable* people were in on this operation. Judges, police, and lawyers were the tip of this iceberg. She shook her head as she stood up straight and stretched her back out.

"I think we're just about done here, girls," Millie said as she walked toward the window facing the street. Bridgette's head rested on the windowpane as she lay asleep on a chair. Millie reached down and shook her softly to wake her. "We can begin loading up our boxes and going through them with more detail and time when we get back home."

Denver picked up a box and nodded. "I'm ready to get out of this house. The memories are hurting my head. And the smell. Like rotten fruit or something. I can't handle it much more."

Millie helped a sleepy, whining Bridgette stand up and picked up her own box when headlights shone into the window.

"Girls, stop," Millie said as she stared at the police car in the driveway, blocking her van.

Bridgette began to cry. "He found us. It's Daddy. He found us!" She screamed as she backed away from the wall and slid down to the floor.

Denver and Sarah crouched to the floor. "That's not Daddy. That is a police officer. Just keep your voices down, and Millie and I will take care of it." Denver said, motioning for the younger girls to hide in the closet. "Sarah. Keep her quiet. I need you two to be strong." Denver said as she followed Millie out of the office.

The front door handle began to twist before the door opened to a uniformed officer standing in the doorway. He stared at Millie and Denver before stepping into the house and shutting and locking the door behind him. In uniform, he stood over the women, light brown hair cropped close to his head. Scars on his face marked his pale skin, one scar cutting down near his eye and another on his lip. Millie slowly reached into the pocket of her loose pants, feeling for the item Amy made her bring with them.

"You ladies are trespassing. What are you doing inside this house?" He said as he pulled a Taser from his utility belt.

"Are you going to arrest us?" Denver asked as she began to shake in fear. Millie looked over at the young girl and back at the officer as he approached them. She sized up the large man as he closed in on them. He was staring at Denver, clearly mistaking her as the bigger threat. Millie smiled as she slowly stepped to the side and watched his approach.

The officer stood directly in front of Denver and grabbed her by the back of her hair, completely disregarding Millie. "I want another taste of your sugar. Roger and Timothy were always so selfish. Didn't want to share his treats, he said. Always wanting more money for just a sample. But Roger isn't here, and it's just me and you. Where are the other two little girls? I have so many ideas of the games we can play."

Memories began to pour into Denver's mind as she stood frozen in the officer's grasp. His face looming over hers, twisted with grotesque pleasure, sweat dripping on her face. His grunting punctuated every sharp, painful thrust on her small body.

Denver remembered now. She was sold to him forever ago before the two younger girls entered the picture. He called it "training her," but for what, she didn't understand at the time; she only knew pain and shame when he was finished with her. Flashes of painful moments played through her memories as she was locked in the moment. He was there in the beginning for all the girls that came through the house for their "training."

He leaned closer and licked the side of her cheek before whispering into her ear. "Of all the virginities I have purchased, you, by far, were my favorite and the most expensive. I wonder if your tears taste as sweet as I remember."

Numbness and rage filled her entire being as she reached behind her for something, anything. Her hands grabbed onto a heavy object sitting on the bookshelf behind her back. Denver wrenched herself from his grasp, ignoring the pain of the hair being pulled from her head, and threw her arms upward, bashing the heavy object as hard as she could against his chin. He grunted and fell to his knees before she lifted the object and smashed the top of his head. His groan and the splatter of warm blood covered her face as she felt herself fall toward the ground with the policeman.

Chapter 14

MILLIE STARED IN HORROR as she watched Denver repeatedly bash the officer over the head with a large, brass bookend. She had the syringe ready in her hand to take the officer down, but the screams of rage froze Millie in place. Blood sprayed into the air, and beautiful displays of a dark red fountain coated Denver as her shrieks brought the sounds of running feet from the office.

Staring at the two young girls as they stared at their sister, Millie was at a loss for what to do. Bridgette, the littlest one, hiccupped with a soft sob, and Denver stopped. She froze with the brass bookend in her hand high above her head. Millie watched as the girls stared at one another. The blank look on Denver's face versus the frozen fear on Bridgette's. She looked at Sarah and the young girl's head was tilted, staring curiously at her sister.

"You did a bad thing," Bridgette whispered to Denver. "Denny, you did a very bad thing."

Denver stood up and held out the brass bookend. "Then why does it feel so good?" She replied. "It feels great. To take back the fear. He hurt us."

Millie watched as Bridgette's eyes widened with realization. Shame, fear, and disgust filled the young girl's face before she covered her features with her hands, crying.

"Take it back, Bridgette. Take it all back. Every touch. Every slap. Each and every single moment, we were used against each other. Take it back." Denver said, motioning with the bookend.

Bridgette slowly walked toward her sister and grasped the heavy object, struggling with the slippery weight. She looked up at Denver and back toward the mutilated face of the dying man groaning on the floor. "He's one of the men that hurt us?" She whispered.

Denver nodded. "I remember now. I had forgotten after so many years, or I just repressed the memories. He paid to break us in. He paid to be the first." Millie watched the heartbreaking moment when Bridgette's eyes widened, and her lip crumbled.

"He hurt me really bad, Denny. I cried, and he told me to cry harder. That he liked my tears. I cried, and he wouldn't stop hurting me. I cried, Denny."

Denver stood up from where she was hunched over the bleeding policeman and waved toward the body. "Make him feel it. Make him bleed."

Millie jumped when Bridgette screamed, throwing herself onto the bloody body, and began to bash the now unrecognizable face with the brass bookend.

"Now, girls. This isn't the way to do this. There are steps we need to take. Girls! I demand you stop right this instant." Millie snapped, trying to break through to the young girl, taking out all her agony on the now dead body.

"I want a turn. Denver, let me have a turn." Sarah said as she walked over toward her sisters and picked up the matching brass bookend from the shelf. Sarah threw herself next to Bridgette, and the girls took turns on the grinded-up hamburger face, his features gone; all that was left was concaved in from the beating by three small girls.

"Girls! I demand you stop this instant. There's an order: we have to clean up DNA; neighbors could hear you. This is not the way to kill someone." Millie said, clapping her hands three times sharply, desperate for them to stop.

All three girls looked up at her, their blonde hair streaked with blood, macabre smiles stretched across their faces, painted red with death.

"We have a lot of work ahead of us tonight," Millie whispered to herself, shaking her head.

Chapter 15

DENVER STOOD IN THE middle of the blood-soaked room, watching as Millie hurried in and out with containers of gasoline. She left her and the other two girls at the house while she drove to the gas station and back, bringing several containers of gasoline with her. She stood back and watched as Millie poured gas all over the dead, stiffening body. The fumes from the fuel began to fill the air, and dizziness filled Denver's head.

"I don't understand what we're doing?" Bridgette asked as she came back inside from the car. Why can't I help in here? Why are you pouring that everywhere?"

Millie shook her head and handed the empty canister to Denver. "We have been here too long. Now, with the extra body here and us walking in and out, we need to destroy any and every fiber of evidence that we were here." Millie walked out of the room with another full-fuel canister and splashed it on the furniture. Denver followed behind her.

"What do you mean extra body?" Denver asked.

Placing the now empty canister onto the ground, she turned toward Denver and shrugged her shoulders. Your Mister is down in the basement, decomposing. I'm surprised no one has discovered it yet. Maybe the cold winter helped to keep the smell from getting too bad. I left a mess behind the day I brought the other two girls home. Now let's get out of here!"

Denver scurried behind Millie as she grasped the arm of Bridgette, who still stood in shock in the middle of the fuel and blood-soaked room. Denver ran with her sister when Millie pulled a lighter out of her pocket, following them out of the front door. Denver opened the van's back door and climbed in behind Bridgette and Sarah, shutting the door behind them and nodding to Millie. She watched as Millie picked up a bottle with a rag stuffed in the top and lit the rag on fire. She began to walk toward the van and threw the lit bottle into the house through the open door, flames engulfing the small home behind Millie. Heat filled her face through the car's glass, red and orange glow reflecting off the van's windows. Mille climbed into the driver's seat of the running van and backed out of the driveway, slowly driving out of the neighborhood.

Denver watched as the past burned; her future was now as bright as the flames that ate at her suffering.

Straightening the last box of files, Denver closed the trunk of the car and walked around, climbing into the back passenger seat. She was surprised at how easily the van sank in the

Buffalo Bayou near where she used to live. She didn't even know it was even that deep. Denver laid her head against the cool glass, shivering as goose bumps lifted on her skin. The night turned cold fast, and Denver didn't have her jacket with her. Sarah lay her head on her lap as they drove down the highway. Amy expertly handled the steering wheel while Millie sat in the front passenger seat, reading some papers from one of the boxes. Denver closed her eyelids, hoping the burn in her eyes from the fire and fumes would soon dissipate.

Denver opened her eyes slightly when she heard Amy whispering from the front seat.

"This needs to end. I supported and helped you in the beginning. But now it's getting out of control."

Denver watched Amy turn on the signal and slow down at the red light before turning right onto an old country road.

"I need to help these girls. The men who abused them are still out there. The man that kidnapped them kept meticulous files on the other men that abused them." Millie shook the paper at Amy. "This guy, for instance. He visited the little one multiple times and hurt her so badly that they had to call a private doctor to administer first aid. I need to find him and give him justice." Millie whispered back before continuing to read the papers.

"I can't do this anymore, Millie. You're choosing those girls over me. And you barely know them. We've been together for years, and you are going to throw us away?"

Millie shook her head. "No, of course not. I love you and don't want to lose you. Maybe I can send these papers anonymously to the authorities."

Denver watched as Amy nodded once. "Good. And the girls?"

"What about the girls?" Millie asked.

"What are you going to do with them? They obviously can't live with us."

Millie shook her head. "I can't throw them into the street. They don't even have identities. They don't have families. I'm not heartless."

Amy scoffed. "Says the woman that has killed over a dozen men."

"That's different, and you know it. I'm not alone in that, either. You helped me with each and every one."

Denver felt the car turn down another road and speed up, gravel pinging at the car's undercarriage. She strained to hear the hushed voices over the noises of the road.

"I know I did, Millie. But this is different. You are investing too much into these girls' lives, and it's time to let go. You are leaving behind evidence that's going to get you caught. And you set fire to a house in a neighborhood. What if it spread? And your van is now at the bottom of the bayou. This is morphing our lives too much, too fast, and not for the better. I hate to be that girlfriend that makes you choose, but it's time. Me or them."

"I thought you liked having the girls around. You told Denver that you would protect her." Millie whispered, her voice heavy with unshed tears.

"That was before your fuckups this evening. These girls are taking away your ability to plan and think. Choose now."

Millie nodded and turned her head to look out the window. "I'll take them to a Houston Hospital tomorrow. Drop them off and leave." She whispered.

Denver closed her own eyes at the end of the conversation as they pulled into the driveway of Millie's house. If Millie had to choose between her and her sisters or Amy, then Denver would be sure to make the right choice for Millie, and it wouldn't be Amy.

Chapter 16

THE KITCHEN WAS EMPTY as Denver sat at the table, nursing a Diet Coke from a can, the cold condensation creating a tingling in her fingers as her hand tightened around the aluminum. She knew Amy would check in on them since Millie had to go into the bar that evening for office work. The smell of the coffee brewing filled the air, and Denver took a deep breath of the comforting smell.

The back door opened with a quiet creek; Amy smiled as she walked into the room and shut the door behind her.

"That smells amazing," Amy said as she picked up a mug from the counter next to the coffee pot and poured herself a cup. "Is there creamer in the fridge?" Amy asked as she scooped sugar into the coffee mug.

Denver grunted and nodded, taking another sip of Diet Coke. "There's some cake too." She said as she slid the plate of dessert over to the empty place setting next to her.

"Oh boy. The best evening snack. Coffee and cake!" Any said as she sat down next to Denver. She watched Amy take a big sip of her coffee, smacking her lips and wrinkling her nose.

"This tastes different. Did Millie get a different brand of coffee or something?"

Nodding, Denver took another drink of her soda. "She said something about trying out the new stock at Brookshire Brothers. I think it was Brazilian or something."

Amy nodded and took another drink before cutting a bite of the cake and eating it. "Mmm, this cake is so delicious. Where did she get the cake?"

"I made it this afternoon. It's just a box, but I ran out of eggs, so I did some research and found that mayonnaise and applesauce can replace the eggs in cake and make it moist. Pretty good, huh?"

Amy nodded and took another bite before taking a big drink of her coffee. "This is amazing. I might have to take a piece up to my room for a midnight snack."

Denver snorted and crushed her now-empty can of soda. "That's probably not going to happen."

Amy looked up at Denver, confused. Standing, Denver looked down at her before she walked over toward the trash to throw away the can.

"I did other research today besides baking and experimenting with ingredients. Millie let me use the computer, and I have been studying a lot."

"Oh?" Amy asked, emptying her coffee cup. She stood up, swaying on her feet as she began to grasp her chest and neck, dropping her cup. The shatter of the mug made Denver jump.

"Did you know that about 600 people a year become sick from Tetrahydrozoline poisoning?" Denver asked from across the kitchen.

Coughing and gagging, Amy fell to her knees on the linoleum floor, trying to crawl toward her bag next to the door. Denver walked over toward her bag and picked it up, setting it on the counter and locking the back door.

"Do you know what Tetrahydrozoline poisoning even is? I mean, you're a doctor. You should be able to tell me."

Nodding, Amy gasped out in a hoarse whisper, "Visine."

Throwing her head back and laughing, Denver lowered herself to her hands and knees so she was right in front of Amy.

"Yes. Visine and nose sprays, too. Did you know that they don't card you when you buy large quantities of Visine from the pharmacy? And that sugar cuts out the bitter flavor of the poison. I find it interesting actually that something that goes into your eyes and nose can be deadly when ingesting large quantities of it."

"Coffee?" Amy whispered as she collapsed to the floor, breathing heavily, her breaths slowing. Denver crawled until she sat next to Amy's head on the floor.

"Yes, the coffee and the icing on the cake. Millie didn't question anything when I told her I wanted to make cake and coffee for you today. She was probably hoping I would butter you up a bit. Make you change your mind about abandoning me and my sisters. Yes, I overheard everything in the car the other night. You really should be sure that when you want to secretly talk about people, they are actually asleep. See, now Millie doesn't have to choose. You chose for her, and you chose me."

She watched Amy's eyes closed as Denver slowly stood up from where she sat next to the woman's head. The door to the living room opened slowly, and Bridgette stood next to Sarah in the entryway.

"Did you have to kill her?" Bridgette asked. "I thought she was nice."

"It was her or us," Sarah said. "We would have been dumped, abandoned to God knows who if Denver didn't do this. We only have each other to protect us, Right Denny?"

Denver nodded. "Only us."

"What are we going to do with the body? It will hurt Millie bad if she finds out that we killed her friend." Bridgette said, wringing her hands nervously.

Smiling, Denver walked over toward the corner of the kitchen and picked up a blanket that she had stored there.

"The neighbors have a pig farm. I read on the internet how pigs will devour anything and everything. I also know he's been out of town for a few days in Houston. Something about a rodeo. So, I thought we could go feed the pigs." Denver said as she spread the blanket onto the floor. "Now, come help me wrap up the body. It will be easier to carry this way."

Sarah shook her head. "You've been reading a lot on the internet lately."

Denver took a pair of scissors from the kitchen drawer, twirling them in her hand as she walked back toward Amy, who was lying on the floor. Smiling, Denver sat on her knees on the floor next to the body. "It's amazing how much you learn from the internet. It was so much faster than the books Mister gave us, too. Now, come help me." As the other girls walked toward her, she used the scissors to cut a lock of the dark brown braid and pocketed it, sliding the scissors across the floor to deal with later.

"What are you going to do with her hair, Denny?" Sarah asked from next to her.

"I'm starting my own collection, of course."

Chapter 17

HUFFING WITH STRAIN AND their breath visible from the cold air, Denver pushed harder at the heavy load they were trying to throw over the wooden fence. She slipped in the mud, nearly falling but succeeding at finally dropping the heavy load over the other side and into the mud.

Looking over at Sarah, she cracked a smile at the smear of mud on the girl's cheek.

"What?" Sarah asked, brushing her hand through her hair.

"You have a bit of mud right there," Bridgette said, pointing to Sarah's cheek.

Denver and Bridgette laughed at Sarah's squeal as she tried to clean off her face with the bottom of her shirt. "This is all your fault,

Denny! You didn't tell me there was mud everywhere."

"I didn't think it would bother you so much. It's just mud." Denver said, laughing as they began their walk back to their house. She shivered as the cold night air hit her sweat-covered body. Amy was a lot heavier than she looked, and it took a lot of work between the three of them to carry her body across the yards to the pig farm. The muddy ground didn't help them either, as they slipped and slid, holding the hefty load wrapped in the blanket.

Squeals began to fill the quiet air, a vicious scream slicing the still and soundless night. Denver looked at Sarah and Bridgette, their eyes wide with wonder.

"Was she not dead?" Sarah asked nervously.

Denver shook her head. "I guess not."

Smiling, Denver turned toward the pig pen as the sound of thrashing mud and screaming began to dissipate. "Should we watch?" Denver asked.

Bridgette and Sarah both smiled back at Denver. "How entertaining," Bridgette said as they turned back and walked toward where they left the woman who tried to ruin them.

Chapter 18

Several days have passed since Amy disappeared. Millie wasn't too surprised that she was gone. Their relationship was starting to fizzle a bit. Millie didn't know if it was because Amy was a doctor, so she was trying to back away from the life of judgment, or if the other woman was becoming bored with their relationship. She disapproved of her bringing home the girls. Maybe she was even jealous of the affection she gave them. She disapproved of a lot of things that Millie was beginning to do. So, her leaving was a little bit of a blessing. But Millie was feeling the loneliness.

The strange thing was that Amy left all of her belongings at Millie's house. She went over to Amy's apartment, but either nobody answered the door or wasn't home. She called the hospital where Millie worked part-time, but they wouldn't tell her anything about Amy either. It was like she just disappeared without a trace and didn't want to have anything to do with Millie. Amy didn't even give her the 24 hours to find a place for her girls. What was she supposed to do, just drop the three young girls at a dog shelter or something?

Millie sat at the kitchen table, sipping her hot coffee as she poured over the paperwork she had removed from the girls' old house. The number of men who visited those three young girls was disgusting. However, the files that were kept on all the men were meticulous. She had names, addresses, times, and dates of visits. Even pictures. She couldn't look at the pictures without vomit gathering in the back of her throat. All these men needed to have justice served.

Millie closed the file as she heard the voices of her girls coming into the kitchen. The door opened, and the three young women walked in. Their clean, brushed, and vibrant blonde hair shined in the sunlight that beamed through the kitchen windowpanes. Dust particles floated in the beams of light, glimmering and dancing around the girls. They laughed at something Denver said as all three of them sat at the table across from Millie.

"You three look beautiful this morning. I can see you healing and changing with time. I'm so proud of you girls."

Sarah blushed and looked down at her lap while Denver cleared her throat, gaining Millie's attention.

"Do we have a new project?" Denver asked.

Millie walked back to the table and took a seat next to Denver. She slid the file over toward the oldest girl and nodded. "His name is Eric. He lives in Houston near the medical center. It's going to be a little difficult to get in and out, but it's doable."

Millie sat back, sipping her coffee as she watched Denver open the file. "Yes, I remember him. He was actually one of the kinder ones.

He didn't leave too many bruises on me. He did like to talk. Quite a bit, actually. I know that he has a family, but he doesn't see them very often. He complained of his ex-wife keeping his kids from him and all the child support he had to pay." Denver closed the file and passed it back to Millie. Sarah stood up and walked toward the toaster, grunting that she was hungry.

Bridgette cleared her voice. "Have you heard from Amy? I miss her."

Millie shook her head. "I'm afraid she's gone, girls. I'm sorry. It's just us. I guess she couldn't handle all my extra baggage. We don't have time to worry about someone who doesn't want to stick around. Let's start planning our in and out. Then we can add to my collection downstairs."

"Collection?" Bridgette asked.

The toast popped, and Millie visibly jumped. "Oh my. That startled me." She said, holding her hand to her heart. "Yes, do you girls want to see my little collection of sins?"

Bridgette smiled and nodded. They walked toward the cold storage door together, leaving the toast untouched on the table.

Chapter 19

Replacing the paper into the file, Denver handed it back to Millie and nodded. "I think you're right. This is probably the best one to visit first." She said. After the tour of the cold storage, Millie sent Sarah and Bridgette outside to play so they could create a plan for their next visit.

Denver was startled at the screaming that was going on outside and stood up. She walked over to the window and peeked through the curtains, smiling as the two younger girls played outside, running around and chasing one another.

"Do you think it's wise that we bring them?" Millie asked as she placed the file folder in her messenger bag on the table.

"I think we should," Denver answered. "I think it might be good for them to see that they aren't in any more danger from the men as we remove them for good. Sarah had another nightmare last night. She's worried about Daddy finding her, and I think if we don't give them this opportunity, she could have nightmares and fear for a while."

Millie nodded. "I see you have been playing on my computer quite a bit lately. Anything interesting?"

Shrugging, Denver replaced the window covering and walked back toward the table. "Just research." She said, sitting back down in her chair.

"Have you thought about enrolling in a school? Maybe get your GED and attend college. You're old enough now."

Tracing her finger over the water stains on the wooden table, she shrugged again. "I don't even know how to go about doing anything like that. I don't have a birth certificate or any identification. None of us do. It's as if we don't exist or we died a long time ago. I searched on the computer for information about myself around the date I was taken, and there was nothing. It's as if I was never reported stolen or kidnapped. I looked for pictures of Sarah and Bridgette, too."

Millie stood up and pushed her chair in. "I'm not worried about identification. I can get that for you pretty easily. Money makes the world go around."

Standing, Denver pushed her own chair in and walked toward the back door. "Well, let's shelve this conversation for later. Robbie isn't going to wait forever for us, is he?"

Millie chuckled at Denver as they walked toward the back door to call in the two other girls. "Robbie" was one of the men on the files they found in the old house. He visited them several times, and it was noted in his file that he kept girls of his own. Millie hoped that was false. She was running out of room with the four of them living together as it was.

Denver came back inside with the girls, and they walked toward the garage together.

Millie didn't have a plan yet, but Denver would have one by the time they got to their destination. Her protegee is becoming quite informative, and Millie looks forward to passing on the mantle. She was excited about the prospect of Denver starting her own collection and being able to watch her grow with knowledge.

Chapter 20

THE CITY WAS SHROUDED in a darkness that was incredibly eerie to Denver. Houston always seemed as if it was alive, lights from homes and buildings shining like the sun, lighting their way down the road. As Millie drove down the near-deserted streets, Denver began to remember times as a little girl, traveling this same route at the same time of night as they were now. She could remember the house they visited and the girls that had forever tear tracks lining their faces, pain evident with every move they made.

Anger filled her chest at the injustice of the young girls who once and probably still suffer at the hands of the men. A sniffle from the backseat had Denver turning around to face the two girls in the car. Bridgette was crying.

"I remember coming here. I didn't like it. They hurt me really bad." She said with tears clogging her throat, her voice thick with anxiety.

"They'll never touch you again. No one will ever hurt you again. I swear on it." Denver said as she nodded and turned back around to face the front. "The men will never hurt another child again." She whispered under her breath.

Shadows of buildings stretched across the road in a macabre display, like hands reaching for their soul, a threatening display of possession for their only worth. Millie expertly pulled into a long driveway, turning off the car's headlights as they drove up to the large house shadowed by the thick live oak trees. She watched as Millie looked down at the paper in her hands, looking happy with Denver's research on the location of the newest acquisition of their collection.

Millie stopped the car behind the house, where the driveway ended, and turned off the ignition. Denver watched as she climbed out of the car and slowly, quietly shut the door.

Denver turned toward the two young girls in the backseat.

"Now, remember to stay near me at all times. We do not separate, no matter what."

She watched as they both nodded. Denver reached into the back seat with both her pinkies held out. "Pinkie swear." She whispered. All three girls clasped their pinkies together and nodded. Denver opened her door and climbed out, quietly shutting it, and opened the car's back door, allowing Sarah and Bridgette to exit. The three of them followed Millie to the back door.

Millie took out a tool pouch from the bag at her side. Denver watched carefully as the woman picked the lock on the door. She knew she had so much more to learn, and watching Millie work was going to be Denver's best teacher. The door opened with a snick, and the scream of the quiet creak that the door made seemed overly loud to her ears.

The humongous house was an open design, the back door leading straight into a kind of sitting room. It was mostly dark, with soft mood lighting creating shadows on the walls. The carpeted floor hid the sounds of their footsteps as Denver followed Millie through the home. She could hardly keep up with Millie as the woman walked quickly through the halls, passing closed doors and walking with a mission. Denver knew what they might find and worried about what it would do to her to witness abuse from someone other than her, Bridgette, and Sarah. Or what it might do to the girls to see such a sight. They were incredibly closed off from the world under Mister's care and were only allowed out on special trips like when they visited here before, though she knew that Mister made sure that there was no one else here but the men who bought them.

Millie stopped in front of a door and placed her hand on the knob, slowly twisting it open. Shrouded in darkness, the bedroom didn't have any visibility. Denver couldn't see anything and wondered how Millie could see in the dark. Two figures lay in the bed, only visible because of the light from the hallway. Denver stood in the doorway as Millie snuck up to the bed. Denver watched as she pulled a syringe from her bag and uncapped the tip with her teeth, sticking the needle in the neck of the man who lay on the bed and injecting the contents into his vein. Denver jumped a little when the man groaned.

She looked over at the young girl lying next to him, her wide eyes open, clouded with fear and pain. Millie nodded toward the wall, and Bridgette reached over to turn on the wall light switch. Denver closed her eyes to the assault of the light, and a whimper prompted Sarah to run toward the girl in the bed.

"Shh, you're okay. We're here to save you." Sarah whispered, brushing the young girl's matted hair from her face. Denver stared at the little girl, who couldn't have been more than ten years old. Blood coated the sheet that covered her tiny body. Her eyes were wide and glassy with shock, with pain. Denver walked over toward the girls, leaving Bridgette to watch them from the door.

"Is there someone we can call?" Denver asked the girl. The little girl jumped as Millie grunted, pulling the now paralyzed man from the bed. The little girl nodded and covered herself up tightly with the sheet.

"My momma. Can you call my momma?" The little girl whispered. Denver nodded and looked around the room. She spied a pair of pants laid over the chair in the corner, and walked toward them. Feeling around the pockets, she pulled out a phone and tried to turn it on.

"It's locked, asking for a fingerprint," Denver said as she walked back towards Millie, who was working diligently on the floor. The other woman held up the man's hand, still attached to the wrist for now, and Denver pressed fingers one by one against the screen until it finally unlocked. She walked back toward the little girl.

"Do you know your mom's number?" Denver asked. The little girl nodded, a hiccup escaping her lips as Sarah cooed and brushed the tears from the girl's face. Denver began dialing when the girl rattled a local phone number.

"Denver," Millie said. She looked up at the woman as the phone in her hand began to ring. Denver handed the phone to Sarah and walked over to where Millie stood over the man on the floor.

"I'm going to go check over the rest of the house. He's not going to be moving for a while. Why don't you and the girls have a little fun."

Denver nodded and smiled as Millie began to walk toward the door. "Oh, and start working on finding out where this girl belongs to. We do not have any more room for any more strays." Millie said, turning back toward Denver.

Denver nodded toward Sarah, who quietly handed the phone over to the crying girl. "Sarah is on it." She said. Millie nodded and left the room, quietly closing the door behind her.

"Bridgette." Denver motioned toward the body on the floor. "Lock the door and come help me. It's time to have a little fun. Payday seems to be on the menu tonight." Bridgette nodded and smiled, locking the door and walking over to where the paralyzed man lay. Sarah lifted the small girl from the bed and walked over to the closet.

Chapter 21

Denver slapped the man's face, waking him from the paralytic. "Ah, there you are. I thought you were going to be sleeping this whole time. It won't stop me from doing what I need to do, but it is more fun that you are able to participate in the games."

She sat back and watched as he looked wildly around with his eyes, unable to move. Fear filled his expression as she began digging in the bag Millie had left behind. A quiet moan had her lifting her head to look at him once again.

"Oh, you have questions, don't you? Well, I'll try to answer them as much as I can." Denver said as she began to pull out the tools of torture; she helped Millie pack. She smiled as his eyes widened.

"You probably don't recognize me. It's been a while since we visited your home. But we remember you. We remember every touch, every bruise. Every moment that we left bleeding. We remember the innocence that was stolen from us and the nightmares that you gave to us. Until we became too old for you, we remember everything that you did, and now, it's time for revenge."

Bridgette giggled as she held up a glass Coke bottle she found under the bed. "Denny, can we use anything on him?"

Denver nodded. "Anything."

She looked back toward the man on the floor. "Do you remember us yet, or has it been too long? I would like to think that we aren't strangers but long-lost friends." More giggling from behind Denver had the man's eyes widen, tears filling his lids and dripping down his cheek.

"Oh, don't cry. It will only hurt for a little while." Denver said as she removed a sharp knife from Millie's bag and traced his naked chest with the tip. "I remember you saying that to me. But I cried anyway. It's okay to cry."

Denver began to cut at his boxer shorts, removing the cotton strips from his groin and thighs. She rolled him over, exposing his naked back to a giggling Bridgette. The man screamed as Bridgette shoved the Coke bottle deep into his ass.

"Denny, I remember when he did this to me. I screamed, too, but he got mad at me and hit me. Should we hit him back?"

Denver shook her head, her ears ringing from the screaming. "No, let him scream it out. We have more mercy than him. He's allowed to scream."

Denver traced the tip of her knife over his scrotum, digging the tip into the skin, watching as droplets of blood began to well up.

"I've been doing a lot of research lately. For instance, did you know that it takes about 50 pounds of pressure to pop a testicle? I've always wondered what it sounds like when they pop.

Do they pop like a balloon, or is it more of an ooze?"

Denver stood up from her sitting position and leaned over the man. "We should find out. I love learning and experimenting. It's the best way to gain knowledge, don't you think?"

She smiled as the man sobbed, slowly shaking his head. "Oh, good. The paralytic is wearing off. Maybe then you might be able to fight a little. I remember you saying you like the fight."

Denver jumped up into the air and landed directly on his penis and testicles, his screams echoing in the small room. Her ears began to ring with the shrill of his cry. Her voice sounded muffled to herself as she spoke.

"You may not remember us from before, but the last thing you will see before you die is our faces. When you enter the gates of Hell, you can tell the others all about Daddy's Little Helpers, and we are coming for the rest of them."

Denver picked up her knife from the floor and slit his neck from ear to ear. Blood spurted in the air as he thrashed and gargled his last breath. She leaned over and pulled a handful of his dark brown hair tight. Using the knife, she sliced a cord of his hair, pocketing it in her pants pocket.

"Is that our trophy?" Bridgette asked.

Denver nodded and stood up. She walked over to the closet where she stashed Sarah and the little girl. Opening the door, she motioned for the girls to come out.

"Did you get a hold of her family?" Denver asked.

Sarah nodded. "I did. They are on the way along with the police. We need to find Millie and clear out of here quickly.

"Denver turned toward the little girl standing in the closet doorway. She was staring at the bloody dead body on the floor next to the bed.

"You didn't see us. You don't know what happened, and you were asleep through it all. Do you understand?"

The little girl nodded. "Is he dead?"

"Yes," Denver answered. "He can never hurt you again."

"I didn't see you. I don't know what happened. I was sleeping in the closet. What about the other girls here?"

Denver sighed and rubbed her hand through her hair. "How many girls?"

Shrugging, the little girl said, "I don't know, but I hear their cries."

"The police and your parents will have to help them. We did what we came to do: serve justice. Just remember, you never saw us."

Denver left the girl in the closet. She picked up Millie's bag and walked toward the bedroom door, with Bridgette and Sarah following close behind her. Denver unlocked the door and walked out into the hallway, nearly colliding with a bloody Millie.

"Are you okay?" Denver asked Millie as she handed the woman her bag.

"Yes, I just found a bleeder. All the men that were here are dead. There are only young girls."

Denver nodded. "A mother called the police. We need to go." The group walked through the hallways the way they came and left through the back door. They quietly and quickly climbed back into the car. Millie started the ignition and began to drive with the lights off. As they turned and exited the driveway and onto the street, Denver looked back at the red and blue lights that turned onto the driveway behind them.

Chapter 22

Cleaning glasses behind the bar, Millie watched her three charges dancing on the wooden floor. She made a mental note to order more clothes for the girls. With a healthy diet and exercise, they are beginning to fill out, and their clothes are starting to be snug. They begin to look happy. Millie noticed that some of their physical scars were also beginning to fade.

A customer walked up to the bar with another drink order, so Millie dried her hands and focused on the customer momentarily, taking the money and clearing the glass after pocketing the tip. She loved this bar that she owned, and The Kenny Store was her salvation. She missed Amy, though, and wished the other woman was here and could see how well the girls looked. Millie thought she could have gotten

Amy to change her mind about letting the girls stay. She didn't know where the 180 came from when, just days before, Amy was just as invested in the girls.

Millie looked back up in search of her girls and began to worry when she couldn't find them on the dance floor anymore. She began searching all over the bar, worry mounting when she couldn't find them.

"Hey, Lou. I need a break. Can you take over, please?" Millie asked her employee as she removed her apron and walked out from behind the bar.

"Sure thing, Millie. It's slow tonight, so take your time."

Walking briskly toward the bathroom, hoping maybe they would go together to relieve themselves, she rushed down the hall. Did their boogey man find them? She began to sweat with worry at the thought of their monster finding them and taking them back to traffic or worse. Millie's chest began to pound and hurt with fear for her girls.

Millie slowed down as she came across the three girls as they faced a doorway to the bathroom. They were watching something, and she cautiously walked up quietly to avoid disturbing them. The three girls were watching a couple kissing in the bathroom. Three heads tilted with curiosity, and the other woman's moans echoed around the small restroom. The couple were so involved with one another that they didn't notice the audience currently watching them.

Heavy breaths punctuated the silent room, sweat glistening off the woman's face, black eyeliner streaking down her cheeks with the silent tears. Her head was thrown back in pleasure, moans escaping her clasped teeth as the man's hand reached under her short skirt, his arm moving in lazy strokes.

"Is he hurting her, Denny?" Bridgette asked in a hushed whisper.

"I don't know. She's not telling him to stop, but she doesn't look like she's enjoying it either. We should stop them. We should kill him and add him to our collection. We can save another girl." Denver pulled a pair of scissors from her back pocket.

Before Millie could stop her, Denver jumped forward and stabbed the scissors into the man's neck, piercing his carotid artery. She yanked the scissors back out, and blood spurted like a heavy fountain, spraying across the girl in front of him. The girl began to scream, her hands flapping against the blood as she tried to back away from Denver.

"Shh, calm down. I saved you." Denver said, trying to placate the girl as she stepped over the dying man, the fountain of blood pouring from his neck now at a slow pump. Denver dropped the scissors onto the floor.

The girl would not stop screaming and tried to run past Denver and the other two girls. Millie grasped the girl by the back of her hair and pushed her head hard into the brick wall of the bathroom, knocking her out cold. Millie then turned back toward Denver.

"What do you think you are doing?" Millie said with her hands on her hips. "I can't leave you alone for a few seconds without you killing someone else?"

Sarah and Bridgette looked at one another before turning back to Millie. "Don't yell at Denver. He was hurting her. Denny saved her. I don't know why she tried to run from us. Denny saved her." Bridgette said.

"Yeah, he was touching her in a private place. She was moaning. We saved her." Denver said with a childlike voice. "I saved her like I want to save all the others."

Millie pinched the bridge of her nose and sighed a long breath. "Girls, they were having sex. She was enjoying it. You can't just go around killing people. We're in a public place. Someone may have heard her scream, or she could have gotten away and called the police."

Millie walked past the three confused girls and kneeled down over the bloody body. "I'm going to have to shut down the bar early tonight to clean up this mess. You girls get started. Lock the door so no one walks in on you. Now I have another body to dispose of." Millie turned back toward the three girls and shook her head. "What do you three have to say for yourselves?"

"Sorry, Millie." They chorused.

Walking back toward the door to the bathroom, Millie turned back toward the girls. "We can't leave any witnesses." She pointedly looked at the knocked-out girl on the floor. "Take care of this mess. I'll be back in a few moments."

Millie started to walk toward the door but changed her mind and turned back to the three girls standing in the bathroom.

"I'll just take these," Millie said, picking up the bloody scissors from the floor.

Millie left the bathroom and waited outside the door until she heard the snick of the lock. Walking toward her storage room, Millie opened the door and reached inside the closet-sized room, pulling out an out-of-order sign. She stomped over to the bathroom and clipped the sign onto the door with the intent to keep people away from the bloody scene.

Stomping in frustration and anger, Millie went back behind the bar and slammed the bloody scissors onto the counter. She poured herself a shot of whiskey and swallowed it down, coughing a little at the smokey taste burning her throat.

"Everything okay, boss?"

Millie turned around and nodded at her employee. "Everything is fine, Lou. The bathroom is out of order. We're going to have to shut down for the night so I can get it working again. Clear out the bar."

She poured another shot and swigged it back as she watched Lou turn off the music and turn on the glaring lights. Millie poured another shot of the whiskey and walked back around the bar to sit on the stool. She took a sip of the liquor and placed the glass down on the wood before hiding her face between her hands. What was she going to do about these girls? They were going to get her into trouble.

"They get on your nerves yet? I know they're hard to handle. It takes someone strong to keep them in line. You were doing pretty good there for a while."

Millie lifted her head and stared at the strange man in front of her. He towered over her where she sat. His piercing honey-colored eyes never wavered from her face. Buzzed blonde hair covered his head. His nose, crooked from too many breaks, wrinkled a little at the smell of the blood. He smiled at Millie, a scar stretching across his upper lip.

"Who are you?" Millie asked, standing from her chair.

The man shook his head. "Tsk, Tsk. I thought you might have known. You did steal all my paperwork and all my files. You can call me Timothy. But my girls all call me Daddy."

Millie's first reaction was to leap onto the bar for the bloody scissors just inches from her. Timothy grabbed her wrist with one hand, slamming it down hard onto the wood. Millie winced with pain and tried to grab the scissors with her other hand, only to be restrained again.

Leaning in close to her ear, he whispered. "Hush now. I think we can come to a little deal. I know quite a bit. More than you, in fact."

Millie leaned her head back and snapped her forehead toward his face, trying to break his nose and tear herself free from his restraining hands. Timothy grunted as he dodged her attempts, pulling her closer into his body.

"Tsk. Tsk. Just as spirited as my little girls." He whispered. "Since they're busy, we have a few moments to talk. I want my girls back." Millie shuddered as she felt spittle run down her cheek from his harsh whispering.

"I want you to go back to your house. Go look through Denver's drawers. That's what she's calling herself now, isn't it?" Millie felt him shake his head with disappointment. She kept her eyes closed and just hoped that he would give her a little give so she could reach for the scissors.

"I do prefer Five. Denver is so redneck and crass." Timothy whispered. "Go look through her collection. You would be surprised by what you find. When you find it, call me, and we can make a deal. You can't handle what they are capable of, and you set free three beasts that can never be tamed."

Millie felt him slide a card into her pants pocket. "Call me, we can make a deal. But I warn you, either way, you want to play this. I will get my girls back."

She fell against the countertop when he pushed her away. Millie reached for the scissors and blindly swiped her hand out, hoping to catch him unaware.

The air was the only resistance to her angry stabs.

Chapter 23

S ITTING IN THE CAR, Millie stared at her house, a dark feeling creeping up her diaphragm. He's been watching her and the girls all this time, knowing where they were and what they all have been doing. The idea of being watched and hunted gave her a disgusted sensation that had saliva collecting in her mouth and throat with nausea. She patted the tight bun on her head, flattening any flyaway hairs before opening the door to her car and climbing out.

The cold air hit her face and cleared her queasiness. Timothy is just trying to cause dissent between her and the girls. She's not going to find anything in Denver's room. What else could be there except for the trophies of the men that hurt the girls?

Millie opened the front door, closed it, and locked it behind her. Her house was completely shrouded in darkness, only the nightlight casting shadows on her wall that screamed with nefarious images dancing in the night. She walked slowly toward Denver's room and opened the bedroom door. Millie had extra bedrooms, but the girls refused to be separated, only wanting to sleep together in the big bed. Clothes were scattered haphazardly around the room, and the bedding was rumpled. She crept toward the chest of drawers across from the bed, opening the first drawer slowly with apprehension. Baby clothes from Dolly were lined in the drawer with reverence as if this drawer were a small shrine to the little girl who lived and died within a week: a bottle and a rattle collected dust in the drawer. A baby blanket was folded neatly.

Millie slowly closed the drawer and began to relax. There's nothing here. She opened the second drawer and then the third. Only clothes and books were in the drawers. Millie turned around to leave but stopped. The closet door was cracked open, and a small shoe box was sticking out. It looked as if one of the girls tried to close the door, but the box was blocking it from being shut all the way. Millie walked over toward the closet and opened it completely. There was nothing in the closet but this small shoe box. Millie sat on the floor and pulled the box toward her, opening it slowly and looking inside.

Bundles of hair lay in the box. All different colors and textures, all tied with twisty ties from her bread loaves.

"Well, that explains what happened to all those ties." Millie laughed to herself. It looked as if the girls had begun their own collection of conquests. Millie went to put the lid back on the box when the light reflected and sparkled off something in the bottom of the shoe box. Millie reached in and pulled out a dark brown braid, shiny beads clasping the thick braid closed.

Millie began to hyperventilate. Reverently stroking the thick braid, she started to cry, rocking back and forth on the floor. Amy's hair was in the box of trophies. At least now, Millie knew what had happened to Amy, that her lover hadn't left her because of her desire to keep the three girls. Unfortunately, it looks as if Denver became jealous and decided to get rid of Amy.

Millie didn't quite understand why. Amy saved Denver's life and the lives of the other two girls. Amy was scared and confused after the fire fiasco, but Millie knew she could talk Amy into not following through with the threat. She wasn't even angry with the two young girls. They follow Denver around and do everything she does. No, this was all Denver.

Millie stood up from the floor and reached into her pocket for the business card. She will let Denver go back to Timothy but will negotiate to keep the younger two girls. They were her girls now. She could teach them and mold them into her new protegees without evil warping their core. Yes, Denver will have to go.

She's just too evil. Millie walked down the hall and pulled her phone out of her purse.

She began to dial.

Chapter 24

MILLIE PULLED THE CAR up to the bar and shut off the ignition. She took a deep breath before opening the door and climbing out of the front seat. Walking up to the back door of The Kenny Store, Millie took a deep breath and unlocked the door.

"Girls? Are you still here?"

The smell of bleach that permeated the bar burned her nostrils, and Millie coughed with discomfort. She walked toward the bathroom and opened the door, surprised by how clean the area was. No trace of blood was left behind. Hearing giggling, Millie followed the sounds of the innocent-sounding laughs toward the front of the bar, where the three girls lay on the wooden dance floor.

"What took you so long to come back? We've been waiting forever." Denver said as she stroked Bridgette's blonde hair, who was lying on her lap.

"I just had a couple of things to do back at the house," Millie said. "What did you do with the two bodies?"

Denver shrugged. "Oh, we fed some farm animals. Didn't we, girls?" The other two began to giggle, their childlike voices giving a chill down Millie's back. Looking down on the floor, Millie noticed muddy footprints dried onto the wood. Looking back at the girls, she noticed the three were covered in mud, and Bridgette was shivering coldly.

"You three look a little muddy and cold. There's a shower in my office bathroom." Millie pointed toward the back of the bar where they could go. "Sarah, why don't you take Bridgette to clean up before she gets hypothermia? I need to talk to Denver real quick."

Millie pointed toward the back door and walked away, expecting Denver to follow her outside. Once the young girl caught up, they walked together toward the tree line behind the restaurant.

"What did you want to talk about, Millie? Do you have another to add to our collection?"

Millie shrugged. "I wanted to talk about what you have been doing with your own collection."

Denver pulled out two cords of hair twisted and tied from the pocket of her jeans. "I thought it was easier to collect hair. No need for jars or preserving."

A branch cracked behind Denver, and Millie looked up, spying on the person behind the young girl.

"Nope, all you need is a shoebox," Millie growled, pulling out the cord of Amy's hair from her pocket. Denver's eyes widened before Timothy hit her over the head and fell to the ground.

Millie looked at the young girl lying in the mud and back at the man, determined to take back his charge.

"We are in accord? The little girls are mine, and you are keeping her."

He nodded and leaned down to pick up Denver, grunting as he threw her over his shoulder.

"Are you going to hurt her?" Millie asked, wringing her hands together.

Timothy shook his head. "Nothing she isn't used to already." He said as he turned and walked away into the darkened trees. Millie heaved a heavy breath and turned back toward the bars with a practiced story to tell the two young girls.

Chapter 25

Denver struggled with the ropes as she slowly woke from her drug-induced sleep. Her eyes struggled to see in the pitch-blackness of the woods. The restraints felt tight against her wrists, her joints and muscles aching from sitting in the chair. She's not sure how long she's been here, but the pain in her body has Denver thinking that it's been quite a while. Goosebumps from the chill in the air rise on her skin as a cold breeze blows her dirty, mangled hair from her face.

Taking a deep breath, Denver began to calm down and think how she was going to get out of this mess. She looked around and noticed how alone she was, feeling grateful that her sisters weren't here with her. The only thing she could remember was the pain of being hit from behind, and she could feel the swelling of a bloody bump on her head. She knew Millie had tricked her and was already planning on how to return the favor, but Denver didn't know why she was out here, alone in the woods.

The crackle of dried leaves on the ground had Denver lifting her head sharply and squinting her eyes in the darkness to see who was walking toward her. The shadow preluded the large man as he stopped in front of her, just out of arms reach. Denver began to laugh.

"What's so funny?" He asked as he took a step backward toward the safety of the darkness.

"You, Daddy. You make me laugh. I'm tied to this chair, unable to move, and you are too scared to come close to me. You couldn't even do the dirty work yourself, could you? Tell me, how did you get Millie to betray me? I was pretty sure she was firmly against you and your 'business.'"

She watched him take a deep breath before speaking. "I told her the truth when I found all of you, how I witnessed you torturing and killing her lover. She was eager to be rid of you and keep the two younger girls for herself, but I plan on taking back my girls before the night is through."

Denver then remembered that last conversation with Millie and how she talked about keeping her trophies in a shoebox. Millie found Amy's trophy.

Denver began to laugh again, spittle running down her face as she cackled, her maniacal laughs echoing in the darkened night.

"Stop laughing!" He yelled, stepping forward and slapping her hard across the face."

Sobering after the slap, Denver spit out blood from the new cut on her tongue. She lifted her eyes to Timothy and quirked one of her eyebrows. "So what's your plan then? Kill me and leave me to die. Then pick up your raping and baby-selling business where you left off?"

Stepping forward, he slapped her hard across the face again. "Shut up! I'll be asking you the questions. How many of my men did you kill? And where are all my girls?"

Denver spit out more blood and shrugged her shoulder. "I don't know where all the girls went. They were never yours and will never be yours again. As for your men... I killed them. I tortured them. They felt what it was like to have no freedom of their body, no voice, no one coming for help, just like the girls that you stole. They felt every single bruise that was placed on us. The lack of power we felt, they felt. They felt every single moment of pain that we felt. I made sure of it before slicing their throats. Just as you will in the moments before your death."

Slapping her again, Timothy pulled a knife out of a sheath and held it to her neck. "I don't think you realize the situation that you are in, my dear. You are tied to the chair. I have a knife to your neck. I have the power to take your life or let you live. But I think I'll make sure you suffer a bit before I decide which way we're going to go. Maybe if you beg me prettily enough, scream for me, I'll let you live to be my fuck toy."

Denver stopped laughing and cleared her throat. "Suffer? Oh, I have already suffered plenty. There's not much else that you can do to me that wasn't already done. Have babies without pain medicine? Done. Burn cigarettes into my skin? Done. Whip my breasts until blood runs down and pools on the floor? Done. Rape me in every single hole my body will allow? Done. You and other men have done it all, and it will take a lot more than you can fathom to bring me to your heel."

Shadows from the clouds covering the full moon fell over them, the dark trees laughing as they swayed in the wind. Branches cracked behind her tormentor, and she began to laugh, covering the sound of the approaching footsteps.

"Stop laughing!" He yelled, pressing the knife tighter against the skin of her neck. Denver could feel the sting of the blade as it began to sink into her.

"You made a good plan here, Daddy. Taking me out here in the woods. Tying me up so I can't get loose. No witnesses. Great plan. But you forgot one little thing."

"What's is that?" He asked as he removed his knife from her neck. Timothy took a step back from her and slapped at his bare arm as a small hand holding a syringe injected poison into his muscle.

"My sisters follow me everywhere. So annoying sisters can be, huh."

Denver watched with a smile as his eyes rolled and fell to the ground. Behind him stood Sarah and Bridgette, their hair tangled from the wind and tears in their eyes, creating clean tracks down their dirty cheeks.

"Boy, am I glad to see you two girls."

"We were scared, Denny," Bridgette said as she picked up the knife Timothy dropped and rushed over to Denver to cut her restraints.

"I was a little scared, too, until I saw your shadows. I knew you were there towards the end." Denver stood up and stretched out her aches, wiping away blood from her face and neck with the cloth that Sarah handed her.

"Can we go home now, Denny?" Bridgette asked.

Denver shook her head. "Not yet. We need to get rid of this trash. Then we need to visit someone that betrayed us."

Sarah nodded. "We are out in the middle of nowhere. We have no tools other than a knife. How do we clean this up?"

Just then, howls began to pierce the quiet night, and Denver smiled, holding out her hand silently, asking for the knife. "We let nature clean up for us."

Chapter 26

MILLIE PACED BACK AND forth in her living room, worry increasing her heart rate with every moment that she hadn't heard from her girls. They weren't at the bar when she returned from the woods, nor were they home, and she had no idea where they ran off to and no way to contact the young women. They were blissfully ignorant of what was out in the world waiting for them, and she worried they would find trouble with having no way to contact her.

She felt a little guilty over Denver, but the girl brought that fate upon herself. The killing was getting out of control. Her killing of Amy was too far. "Too much damage." She whispered to herself as she stopped pacing.

A heavy knocking had Millie rushing toward the front door, swinging it open wide and gasping in shock at a disheveled and bloody Denver standing on her front porch. She held a knife in one relaxed hand, her arm swinging slightly near her waist. Blood leaked from her mouth and neck, dripping onto the foyer as the young girl pushed past her and into her home.

"Denver? What? How?"

The other two young girls blocked Millie from leaving through the door and stepped into the house as well.

"What's going on?" Millie asked as Bridgette shut the door behind them, locking the deadbolt.

Denver smiled, blood coating her once-white teeth. "Revenge," she said as she leaped forward with the knife.

The End